PIZZA, Love, and Other Stuff That Made Me Famous

Other great reads you may enjoy

52 Reasons to Hate My Father
Jessica Brody

Flirt Club
Cathleen Daly

Just Flirt
Laura Bowers

The Karma Club
Jessica Brody

My Invented Life
Lauren Bjorkman

My Life Undecided
Jessica Brody

Paradise
Jill S. Alexander

The Poison Apples
Lily Archer

The Stalker Chronicles
Carley Moore

Wicked Sweet
Mar'ce Merrell

Kathryn Williams

PIZZA, Love, and Other Stuff That Made Me Famous

SQUARE FISH

Henry Holt and Company — NEW YORK

SQUARE FISH

An Imprint of Macmillan
175 Fifth Avenue
New York, NY 10010
macteenbooks.com

PIZZA, LOVE, AND OTHER STUFF THAT MADE ME FAMOUS.
 Printed in the United States of America by
R. R. Donnelley & Sons Company, Harrisonburg, Virginia.

Library of Congress Cataloging-in-Publication Data
Williams, Kathryn.
Pizza, love, and other stuff that made me famous / Kathryn Williams
p. cm.
"Christy Ottaviano Books."
ISBN 978-1-250-02745-0
[1. Cooking—Fiction. 2. Reality television programs—Fiction. 3. Television—Production and direction—Fiction. 4. Interpersonal relations—Fiction. 5. Competition (Psychology)—Fiction. 6. Restaurants—Fiction.] I. Title.
PZ7.W6665811437Pi 2012 [Fic]—dc23 2011034053

Originally published in the United States by
Christy Ottaviano Books/Henry Holt and Company
First Square Fish Edition: August 2013
Book designed by April Ward
Square Fish logo designed by Filomena Tuosto

10 9 8 7 6 5 4 3 2 1

AR: 5.2 / LEXILE: 780L

For Hugo, who always eats his peas

PIZZA, Love, and Other Stuff That Made Me Famous

Chapter One

My mother's recipe for tomato sauce starts with ripe plum tomatoes. To peel them, you use a sharp knife to cut a tiny *X* in the skin at one end. You dunk them in boiling water, just for a second—maybe ten—and run them under cold water. Then you pull back the skins, just like peeling a banana. You crush the tomatocs with your hands and stew them over low heat in their own juices with garlic, onions, and a bay leaf that have been sautéed in extra-virgin olive oil. Dash in some salt and pepper, and there you have it. The smell is nothing short of heaven.

My father says this tomato sauce was the first thing my mother mastered in the kitchen. He likes to add oregano and basil and more garlic—always more garlic. I never knew my mother, but I know this recipe by heart. I have it displayed in a five-by-seven, plastic craft store frame on the desk in my room, the desk where I'm supposed to do homework but can't because it's covered in books and dirty clothes. The recipe is written on an unlined index card. It's stained with oil splatters, and one corner's ripped. I realize framing a recipe for tomato sauce sounds strange, but it's a reminder, not just of my mother but that every cook has to start somewhere.

It was Saturday night, and I was doing what I'd done every Saturday night since I was ten: rolling silverware in the empty dining room of my family's restaurant (Taverna Ristorante, est. 1997). I raced through it—napkin, fork, knife, spoon . . . roll . . . napkin, fork, knife, spoon . . . roll—the rhythm so deeply ingrained I could do it with my eyes closed. My rush was only partially motivated by boredom. I also wanted to get where I really belonged—in the kitchen. Napkin, fork, knife, spoon . . . roll. Done. Finally. Eighty red linen eggrolls sat stacked in two neat pyramids on the white tablecloth in front of me.

"Dad!" I shouted at the water-stained ceiling festooned with fake grapevines. I knew he could hear me in the office upstairs. "I'm going to help Luís in the back!"

Only when I swung through the double doors into the brightly lit, bustling kitchen could I remember why I actually loved working at the restaurant. The kitchen was alive.

"Hot pan, comin' through!" someone yelled. Quickly, I sidestepped a potentially disastrous encounter with a sheet pan of steaming moussaka.

"Sophie," Carlos said, high-fiving me. "How are you this evening, *chiquita*? *¿Qué pasa?*"

I sighed. "*Nada, Carlos. Mi vida es totalmente aburrida.*"

I loved the word for "bored" in Spanish because it sounded like "a burrito."

My family opened Taverna Ristorante in the Georgetown neighborhood of Washington, DC, when I was three. The name was a nod to my father's Greek-Italian heritage. My grandmother is Italian, from Orvieto, and my grandfather is Greek, from Thíra. The year after they opened the restaurant, my mother died of a sudden and unexplained brain aneurysm while folding clothes on an otherwise ordinary day in the northern Virginia suburb where we live. I don't remember this, of course—I was four.

I have few memories of my mother, mostly just vague images of playing at her feet on our kitchen floor. My older brother, Raffi (short for Raffaello and, yes, pronounced the same as the children's singer), was the one who told me the details of my mother's death years later. I wasn't sure how much I could trust him, though, because he also told me I was adopted. I had cried until my father brought down a photo album from the bookshelf above our television. He turned its yellowed pages until he came to a faded snapshot of a beautiful blond woman looking not at the camera but at the pink-hatted baby cradled in her arms. An olive-skinned young man beamed at the camera beside her, as if to say, "Look, Ma! I made a baby!"

"How do I know that's me?" I'd asked with a still trembling lip. "Or that you didn't stage it after you adopted me?" My dad muttered something in Greek and took Raffi's Xbox away for three days.

With the help of my grandparents, Taverna Ristorante survived. It was my home. I'd been working legally there since I was thirteen. Only when I turned sixteen did my dad agree to hire a hostess and let me go where the real action was—on the line.

Anyone who enjoyed Taverna Ristorante's traditional Mediterranean cuisine might have been surprised to find that the kitchen staff was overwhelmingly Hispanic. Our head chef, Luís, was Portuguese, but he spoke Spanish too. It exasperated my father that I couldn't speak enough Greek to find a bathroom and only enough Italian to order a pizza Margherita, yet I was proficient *en español*, with a pretty decent grasp of the language's culinary terms (to broil = *asar a la parilla*).

After washing my hands at the small sink in the corner of the kitchen, which ran water that was invariably scalding or ice cold, I grabbed my apron off the hook by the door. It was a birthday gift from Alex. It said STAND BACK! GRANDPA IS GRILLIN', an inside joke from the time Alex tried to cook dinner for me for once. We'd ended up eating chips and burger toppings. Ketchup on top of a Dorito, while not especially palate-challenging, is surprisingly good.

The apron was stupid, but it made me laugh. Alex could always make me laugh. He was my best friend. He was also a boy. Until recently, I hadn't seen a conflict between those two attributes. Until recently, I hadn't imagined what it would be like to kiss him. It was becoming increasingly inconvenient.

"What can I do, Luís?" I asked. Carlos was Luís's sous-chef, but I was his right-hand girl. I was in charge of prepping ingredients for the daily specials.

Thwack—the flat side of Luís's knife crushed a clove of

garlic against the cutting board. "Tonight," he announced with a flourish, "we are featuring a lasagne primavera with yellow squash, portobello mushroom, and ricotta."

I liked how Luís rolled words around in his mouth as if he was tasting them. He always made a big production out of his specials—maybe because they were the only thing he controlled on the menu. The rest of it was composed of Greek and Italian classics, mostly recipes my father inherited from Nonna and Pappou, who had owned a restaurant back in Thíra. Taverna Ristorante was more spaghetti carbonara than wasabi and panko-crusted skate with lime chervil salsa. My dad liked to say, "Not fine dining—great dining!" Painful.

"Mmmmm." I stuck a spoon into a pot of marinara bubbling on the six-burner stove and tasted. "Needs more garlic." Carlos playfully batted my hand away with a charred oven mitt.

I liked working with Luís. He knew I wanted to be a chef when I grew up, and not just a chef, but a top chef. He didn't laugh when I talked about "flavor profiles" and "balance." Sometimes he even took my advice, dashing in a little more salt or coriander when he thought my back was turned.

"Where can I start?" I asked, running my hands down the sides of my apron.

"Onions," said Luís, only it sounded like *own-yuns*.

"Aye-aye, cap'n." It was cry time.

By six, the dining room was nearly full with early birds—old people and families with small children, who left almost nonexistent tips and a sprinkling of bread crumbs around their tables like Hansel and Gretel scattering a trail out of the forest. The waitstaff hated the early birds, but my father loved them. He loved every customer, but particularly those who, like him, saw meals as a ritual. For Antonio Nicolaides, food was about family and community as much as it was about taste and nourishment. Which was why you could find him every night circling the dining room like a nervous socialite, chatting with customers, asking how their meals were or, if they were regulars, inquiring about their hip replacement surgeries and recent Disney vacations.

"Order up!" yelled Luís.

The doors to the kitchen thwapped open and closed for Nikki, a waitress who'd been with us as long as I could remember. She was from Greece, which made her family. She whisked two hot plates of moussaka from the window. I wondered how she hadn't burned all the skin off her fingers yet, but she refused to use a tray.

"And eighty-six the bucatini!" Luís yelled after her, meaning we were out of it.

Nikki cursed. "Okay. Hold my order on table ten till I can see what Mr. Meinhardt wants instead."

As she backed through the door, I glimpsed my father in the dining room. He was talking to table eight, where the Tuccis' four boys were polishing off a mountain of spaghetti and meatballs. The door swung open again, and I caught his baritone voice, still stubbornly accented after all these years. He was mid-story.

"Oh, geez." I wiped the seeds of the tomato I was chopping into a food scraps bin.

"*Cómo?*" asked Pablo. He was one of the line chefs tearing lettuce for salads beside me.

"He's telling it again."

Pablo and Carlos chortled, and Carlos launched into his near-perfect imitation of my father. "Sophia, my daughter, she's the real cook in the family. When she was three years old—just a baby!—she baked a chocolate soufflé in her Easy-Bake Oven. Her mother was reading Julia Child—"

I had to cut Carlos off. I'd heard my father tell the story of my preadolescent culinary genius a thousand times. I knew our customers had also; they were just too polite to stop him.

The flow on Saturday evenings was always the same. The six-o'clock crowd was replaced gradually by the eight-o'clock crowd—young professionals and couples on dates, who liked to linger over their meals. They ordered desserts to share and bottles of wine as the grumbling servers loitered by the cash register tucked behind a lattice decorated with more fake grapevines. My father didn't like our diners to see their orders being put into the computer or their bills being printed. He preferred things to just appear on the table, as if willed into being by Zeus himself.

I did the math once. In four hours, we would put out approximately 172 entrees, 57 appetizers, 193 baskets of bread, and 36 desserts—or 0.716 meals per minute. In other words, don't think, just cook. And so my Saturday nights sped by in a marathon of chopping, peeling, plating, and—the best part—tasting.

By nine forty-five, my feet were aching in my clogs and

my head was buzzing with the heat and energy of the kitchen, but the tickets on the line had dwindled to five. We were almost there.

Carlos, a kitchen rag slung over the shoulder of his marinara-splattered chef's jacket, stood on his tiptoes, peering out the porthole-shaped window in the door to the dining room. "Your boyfriend's here!" he yelled across the kitchen.

The eyes of a dishwasher named Ramón darted to me. I could often feel them on the back of my head. It was a running joke in the kitchen that Ramón was madly, Mexican-soap-opera-style, in love with me. Lucky for Ramón, he didn't speak enough English to know his tortured love kept the entire kitchen entertained through dinner service.

"He's not my boyfriend," I said quickly, but I could feel myself blushing. "He's my friend who happens to be a boy." I hated that the teasing in the kitchen about Alex had suddenly started to embarrass me. Worse, I hated that I couldn't hide that it did.

"Maybe you should tell him that, because he's hanging around like *un perro*," said Carlos, making puppy-dog eyes.

I had been artfully topping a tiramisù with whipped cream. I pushed it to Pablo, wiped my hands on my apron, and peered out the window, narrowly escaping a concussion as a waiter flew through the door. Alex was standing at the hostess stand, but he looked nothing like a lovesick puppy to me. He was chatting with Amber, our new hostess, a grad student working her way through Georgetown Law. I wasn't sure yet if I liked her. Considering the way she was playing with her hair as she talked to Alex, the forecast was a ninety percent chance of no.

Alex leaned over the hostess stand and pointed at something on a piece of paper. His blond bangs flopped over one eye. Despite my repeated objections that he looked like a certain tween pop star, Alex refused to cut his hair. It was too long and always fell in his eyes, which in my opinion were his best feature. They were a bright, almost jade green, like cat eyes, with a ring of brown around the edges. . . . Not that I spent a lot of time gazing into them or anything. His surfer hair worked for at least one girl, though—a freshman named Lindy who kept finding far-fetched reasons to hang out by Alex's locker. I did not care for Lindy.

I pulled my apron over my head, adjusted the baseball cap I had to wear for health codes, and exited the fluorescent kitchen into the relative murkiness of the dining room.

"Soph!" Alex's eyes lit up the way they did when he wanted something from me.

I narrowed mine suspiciously in return. "Hey. Kind of in the middle of something. What's up?"

"It couldn't wait."

"What couldn't wait?"

"The contest."

"What contest, Alex?"

Alex held some kind of application up to my face. "*Teen Test Kitchen* Qualifying Competition," I read at the top.

I took the paper and squinted down at the small print. Glasses would just not look right perched on my big, fat

Greek nose, and I couldn't even begin to think about touching my eyeballs every day. "What is this?" I asked.

Alex had a big, sloppy grin on his face that happened to show off his annoyingly cute dimples, and he was shifting his weight from foot to foot. "It's your Golden Ticket." He tapped the top of the page. "You're welcome."

I gave him a look that said, "I have four tiramisùs and what are probably now two bowls of gelato soup waiting for me in the kitchen."

Alex snatched the paper from my hands, waving it in frustration. "It's a reality show cooking competition thing. And you're going to win it."

I laughed as if Alex had just announced my nomination for homecoming queen—a fun fantasy but entirely implausible. "I'm going to win it?"

"Yep." His eyes sparkled with an intensity I had no power against.

That was the sparkle that had been getting me into trouble since third grade, when Alex's mom, then just a random neighbor, invited me to the Underhills' house. She wanted me to give my chicken pox to her son. On the phone with my dad, she called it a "chicken pox party." My dad called it "strange" but allowed me to go anyway. It was after lunch when Alex convinced innocent, young, calamine-covered me that we were going to run away together, preferably to the circus, but not the kind where they were mean to animals. We had stolen his mom's keys and gotten as far as the end of the driveway with the gearshift in neutral before Mrs. Underhill ran out of the house screaming.

I cocked an eyebrow and spoke in a mockingly soothing voice. "Hey, Alex, have we made an unscheduled stop in Absurdistan? Because I didn't see it on the itinerary."

Alex and I had had sixth-grade geography together and found it nearly impossible to recite the "-stan" countries in front of the class without cracking up. It thereafter wormed its way into our private lexicon. Rather than Uzbekistan, people in our world lived in Freakistan and Creepistan. If they were particularly insufferable, they carried passports from Turdistan.

A sudden clang of metal followed by the sound of china shattering on a tile floor exploded from behind the kitchen doors. Our few remaining patrons swiveled their heads toward the sound.

"I gotta go," I said. "You're staying for dinner, right?"

"Of course, *principessa*." I suspect he said it with a dorky flourish, but I wasn't sure, as I was already halfway to the kitchen with my dad on my heels.

When the OPEN sign on the front door was flipped to CLOSED, the Nicolaides family and whatever staff had stuck around would sit down for a meal in the Taverna Ristorante dining room. If your last name was Nicolaides and you resided at 1802 Springfield Drive in Fairfax, Virginia, you had to be at family dinner. It was not a choice; it was a duty. And not just on Saturdays either, but Fridays too. I blamed my complete lack of a social life on these dinners.

Raffi had somehow convinced Dad to give him the night off work for a "school concert" I suspected was anything but. He rolled in at half past ten. The chairs were already up on the tables. He helped Nikki and another waiter named Dave pull together some four-tops to make one long table in the center of the restaurant. Alex and I set out platters of spaghetti, salad, and what was left of Luís's very popular lasagne primavera. My dad was in the office entering credit card receipts and locking the night's cash in the safe. We finally heard his heavy footsteps on the old, creaky stairs.

"*Baba, buenas noche!*" Alex cried as my father appeared. He threw his arms open in an exaggerated, Mafia-family–style hug.

"I am not your baba, Alex," said my father, forgoing the hug for a rough tousle of Alex's shaggy blond hair instead. The scene was well rehearsed. Dad had never totally gotten over his suspicion of the boy his daughter vehemently claimed was just a friend (he still wasn't allowed in my room), but I knew he loved Alex.

My father took his usual seat at the head of the table. The rest of us, a dozen or so, filled in, and before long, the conversation and wine were flowing. These dinners often lasted two, once even three, hours, until line cooks had to get home to wives and children and waitresses had to meet their boyfriends. After his dramatic entrance earlier, I was amazed that Alex made it almost thirty minutes before bringing up the application again. I tried to distract him with seconds and thirds, but at some point, a boy gets full.

"So," he said, and I knew it was coming. He leaned back on the legs of his chair and threw an arm around Raffi's seat next to him. "How do you guys feel about reality TV?"

I sent an expeditious elbow to his ribs. "Ooof." He winced.

Raffi gave us a look that said, "Remind me again why I converse with you," and I was suddenly glad my brother didn't care to pay me too much attention. "You mean those shows where twenty hot girls fight over one douchey guy?" he asked.

"Douchey?" my father echoed from the end of the table. He was deep in conversation with Luís, probably about something really fascinating like ramekins or Saran wrap, but he had a superhuman ability to listen to multiple conversations at once.

"Sorry," said Raffi. He rolled his eyes and popped a briny brown olive into his mouth, then spit the hard pit into his hand. "Dorky."

"I mean the competition ones . . . like the ones with cooking." Alex was ignoring the incendiary laser beams I was directing at him with my eyes like Drew Barrymore in *Firestarter.* I had a huge girl crush on Drew Barrymore—not the romantic kind, but the I-want-to-be-you kind.

Raffi shrugged a half-interested shoulder and expelled another olive pit.

"He doesn't care," I replied for him.

Amber said something about a new bar in the neighborhood, or maybe the bar exam, and Raffi turned his attention to her.

"Why are you being so weird?" Alex whispered.

"I'm not being weird. I just don't need you to bring it up in front of them." I nodded toward my overprotective father and supremely annoying brother. "I don't even know what it is yet!"

"It's a reality show for teen chefs, and it's your chance,

Soph. Your once-in-a-lifetime chance." We were still whispering.

"Alex, there is no way I'm going to win a game show, or get on a game show for that matter."

"It's not a game show; it's a reality competition."

"Excuse me. Whatever. . . . Can we just talk about it tomorrow?"

"Sophie—" Alex started, but, thankfully, my dad interrupted from the other end of the table. He was asking me to fetch the world-famous Nicolaides family recipe book from the office. It was a tattered, homemade cookbook that Nonna handed down to my father, just as her mother had handed it down to her. Most of it was in Italian. I jumped to get it.

My grandparents used to attend these family dinners but were coming to the restaurant less and less now, which seemed only to make my brother's and my attendance more mandatory. I knew I'd come home to find Pappou asleep in the wing chair in the living room, the TV turned up to a squawk. My father would wake him and help him to his room, where my grandmother was already sleeping.

By the time we cleared and cleaned up and my father locked the door behind us, it was past midnight.

"Good night," I called to Alex's silhouette retreating toward his car in the glow of the Georgetown streetlamps. A twinge of guilt was growing in my chest for shooting down his idea. He seemed so genuinely excited about the prospect of this *Teen Test Kitchen*. How did he have such confidence in me? I wondered.

"Good night, Alex!" my father called.

"Good night, Mr. Nicolaides!" Alex raised a hand in a backward wave. "Thanks for dinner. *Thavma* as always!"

My dad chuckled at Alex's butchered Greek. *Thavma* means "marvelous," but more closely, "miraculous." My father had never corrected him.

I was being lulled into a pleasant food coma in the passenger seat of my father's car when my cell phone beeped. I already knew who the text was from. Think about it. Of course I would. I just didn't want to get my hopes up. I loved to cook—I wanted to show the world I could cook—but I thought I'd have a little more time before I got my shot. A reality show launching me into culinary stardom sounded like something of a miracle, but up till now, Sophie Nicolaides's life hadn't been so *thavma*.

"Good morning."

"Seriously?" The phone was pressed to my ear, but my eyes were still closed. Alex, the early riser, knew I had a strict no-calls-before-noon rule on weekends.

"It's the voice of reason calling. We have some matters to discuss. Matter one: getting you on television."

I groaned and rolled over to look at the clock. It was nine thirty. My dad had been awake for four hours. "I don't want to be on TV, Alex."

"But you do want to be a world-famous chef, and I don't see the *New York Times* restaurant critic banging down the door of Taverna Ristorante. No offense."

"None taken."

"You need a platform, a springboard if you will."

"I will."

"Here's the plan: You get on *Teen Test Kitchen*. You showcase your sparkling wit, general fabulosity, and near-genius abilities with food. You win over America. You open your own restaurant in New York, and you hire yours truly as general manager."

"Fabulosity? Are you sure you're not gay?"

"I'll take that as a compliment."

I pushed the heels of my palms against my eyelids. "Fine. Let's pretend for a split second that my dad is not the strictest father inside and outside the Beltway, and that I decide to take this little trip to Ridiculously-Out-of-My-Leagueistan. What exactly does this competition entail?"

Alex read from the casting call. "From the producers of *Chop Shop* and *Catwalk* comes a new Food TV reality show to find America's next generation of culinary talent. *Teen Test Kitchen* will bring eight of America's most promising young chefs to Napa Valley"—Alex paused for that detail to soak in—"for seven weeks of classes and competition at the country's premier culinary institute, the National Culinary Academy." Another pause for effect. "The winner will receive a full scholarship to the NCA and a coveted apprenticeship with judge-producer, top chef, and restaurateur Tommy Chang."

"Tommy Chang?" I tried not to sound excited by the prospect of meeting one of the world's most accomplished chefs. It was like telling a kid she'd meet Santa Claus at the Easter Bunny's house—if she could pull a rabbit out of her hat.

"*The* Tommy Chang," Alex said.

I bit my lip. It did sound too good to be true. But seven

weeks? That was almost the whole summer. I couldn't help but feel a little disappointed that Alex seemed to have no problem shipping me off to California. I'd been looking forward to our summer together; we'd already planned a road trip to the Chesapeake Bay. "Are you trying to get rid of me?" I teased.

"Sophie," Alex said, getting as serious as I'd ever heard him. "You have a real talent—I've tasted it. Here's your chance to be discovered. You just have to cook one great dish. What do you have to lose?"

"You're not letting go of this, are you?"

"Nope. I'm stuck like white on rice, baby."

I was scared, but there was also a tiny voice in my head getting louder by the second screaming, "What are you waiting for?"

I stared at the water stain shaped like a duck on my ceiling. Besides being home to the NCA, Napa Valley was where my aunt Mary owned a restaurant. My mom's sister had been a fixture in our lives for a while after my mom died, bringing over food and taking Raffi and me to the zoo, but she moved to California when I was nine to start her own restaurant. Even as a kid, I could tell my dad was angry she left us. Family was everything to him. I hadn't seen her since then, but she sent me postcards and birthday gifts from the crazy places she traveled: a handmade bowl from the Yucatán Peninsula, a necklace from Morocco, a dashiki from West Africa. As far as I could tell, my aunt was a globe-trotting hippie.

"Okay," I said. "I'll do it. But you have to agree to be my taste tester."

"As your friend, I accept that burden," said Alex.

"How do you feel about lamb?"

"I feel good about it."

"When are the tryouts?"

"Next weekend."

"That's not much time."

"It's enough. You're ready for this, Soph."

Already I was mentally rifling through the two-foot stack of my mother's old cookbooks, which served double duty as both bedtime reading and nightstand. I would never win, I knew, but I would make a damn good meal trying.

My Mother's Tomato Sauce

This simple sauce was my mother's recipe—the one I keep framed on my desk. It's best with summer-ripe tomatoes, but you can use whole canned tomatoes too. I've added the oregano and basil my father likes to include. He's also been known to sneak in an extra garlic clove—or three. It's great served with any kind of pasta or even poured over roasted or grilled zucchini and eggplant.

MAKES 3 CUPS (enough for 4 people over pasta)

Ingredients

2 pounds ripe plum tomatoes, peeled
3 tablespoons extra-virgin olive oil
2 small white or yellow onions, finely chopped
1 bay leaf
2 cloves garlic, minced
1 teaspoon fresh oregano leaves, finely chopped
1 teaspoon fresh basil, finely chopped
Kosher salt and freshly ground black pepper, to taste

Directions

1. Heat olive oil in a large pot over low heat. Add onions and bay leaf and cook slowly, stirring occasionally, for 10 minutes, or until onions are soft and translucent. Add garlic to the pot and stir well.

2. Crush the peeled tomatoes in your hands over a bowl (you want the tomato pieces to be uneven and chunky). Add tomatoes to the pot, stir, and let simmer for 45 minutes, stirring occasionally. Remove the bay leaf. Stir in oregano and basil, then season with salt and pepper. Always taste to see if it could use more salt or spices (remember, you can add more, but you can't take it out).

Chapter Two

According to Alex's count, there were fifty-seven contestants in line, not including parents.

"I have to pee," I whined, bouncing at the knees. Alex was used to ignoring comments like these—anything about being hot, cold, or having to pee. Only girls talk about that stuff, he told me; guys just do something about it.

To be safe, Alex made us arrive an hour before the time listed in the casting call. "I hardly think the Marriott is going to be stormed by a flash mob of teen chefs," I'd responded to his wakeup call. Apparently I was wrong.

We had to do some quick thinking to explain to my dad why we were leaving my house at seven thirty in the morning, when I normally didn't emerge from the dragon cave of my room until at least eleven. Why concern him, I figured, when I wasn't going to win anyway? I was saving us both an argument. I was doing him a favor, really. Alex and I had come up with the cover of a soccer tournament he was dragging me to. My dad loved soccer, or "football," as he insisted on calling it, so he asked no more questions. The excuse also accounted, somewhat, for the cooler filled with ingredients for the dish I'd be making for the try-out: rosemary lamb chops with white bean ragout. "Snacks," I'd explained as I carried the cooler through the kitchen past my father. "Olé, olé, olé!" he'd cheered. Like stealing candy from a baby—I almost felt bad.

The Marriott was a zoo. Besides the casting people and a radio station playing nonstop pop hits from a van, there was a TV news truck. Afraid my cover would be blown by *News4 at 6*, I dodged the panning lenses of the cameras and avoided eye contact with reporters. It wasn't hard, trying to appear camera shy. I freaked out when I realized the day's top ten chefs would have to do an on-camera interview.

"Alex, I'm boring."

"No, you're not. Just tell them about your family and the restaurant, and stress the Greek-Italian thing." He made a *Godfather*-esque brush of his chin. "You've got a father who hangs garlic in his room for good luck and grand-parents who speak in dead languages. That's television gold, my friend."

"They're not dead if people speak them."

"Whatever. It's gotta be worth something. Oh, and make sure you include the part about your mom. Producers love a sob story."

"Be careful—your sensitive side is showing," I said. I

was not about to use the memory of my late mother to get onto a reality show, Tommy Chang or no Tommy Chang.

The casting call said participants must be between the ages of fifteen and eighteen at the start of filming. As I looked around I wondered if a few of the kids in line had birth certificates to back that up. One girl, standing next to a perfectly shellacked stage mom, looked not a day over eleven. There were boys and girls of all shapes, sizes, and ethnicities. I saw my Greek-Italian edge go up in a puff of grill smoke. I only wished I had X-ray vision to peek inside the coolers they'd brought with them. I had a hiccup of fear that my rosemary lamb chops wouldn't be the only ones on the judges' table.

Alex returned with a fresh application. I'd tried to fill the last one out on my knee, but was so nervous I poked through the *N* in my name, jabbing my leg with the pen.

"Where am I supposed to fill this out?" I wondered, finding no more reliable writing surfaces.

"Here." Alex turned and offered me his back to lean on. Sometimes it felt weird to touch Alex. I mean, we'd touched—not in *that* way—a million times before. But recently, something was different. Like when his finger brushed accidentally against mine, or like the week before, when he'd put his hands over my eyes in the hall at school—it made me nervous. Alex was my friend, who was not short but not tall either, with too-long hair and occasional eczema. So why did leaning on his back make me light-headed? Just concentrate, I commanded myself, and don't give him a puncture wound.

When I reached the permission page, where a guardian

was supposed to sign, I eyed the people around me nervously. They were preoccupied with their own applications and conversations. "Alex," I whispered. He turned his head, and I discreetly slipped the form and pen into his hand. In a half second, he'd dashed off a signature that actually resembled my father's for the simple reason that Dad's handwriting looks like the scribble of a rabid, left-handed chicken.

"There," Alex said out of the side of his mouth.

"Thanks," I replied the same way. My father would kill me.

I flipped to the first page and started to reread my answers for the fourth time.

"You're nervous, aren't you?" asked Alex. I looked at him. "Stupid question," he said. His bangs had fallen into his eyes again, and he flicked them off his face with a spastic shake of his head. I went back to reading my answers.

Someone with a headset and what looked like a walkie-talkie finally swung through the double doors, teasing us with a glimpse of a ballroom full of gleaming kitchen equipment. A woman introduced herself as the casting director and ran through the rules of the competition. The chefs would have ninety minutes to prep, cook, and plate four servings of a dish of our choosing. It could be anything—an entrée, an appetizer, a dessert, a side, breakfast, lunch, dinner—it just had to taste, and look, good. She instructed us to hand our applications to another woman wearing a headset named Kim, who smiled and waved.

"Confirm your full name and age and proceed to the

cooking station labeled with the number you were given when you checked in. Good luck."

The room felt huge, easily the size of an airplane hangar, and was lined with rows of cooking stations. Each station was equipped with an oven, a mini fridge, and a small countertop. It was cold with the air-conditioning on in March, but I suspected it was about to get very hot.

As Alex helped me unpack the ingredients for my dish from the cooler, I took stock of my station. Cutting board. Check. Knives. Check. Bowls. Check. Can opener. Check. Lucky apron. Check. Oven and stove. Obviously check.

I opened the bottom drawer of the oven. There were two metal cookie sheets. I stood and frowned.

"What's up?" Alex reached around me to set a Ziploc of fresh rosemary on the cutting board.

I ducked down again and peered into the oven drawer. My heart stopped. "There's not a broiler pan!"

"What's a broiler pan?"

"It's the thing I have to cook the lamb chops in!" My voice was getting louder and shrill. Alex knew this voice and knew that this voice meant Watch for Oncoming Freak-Outs. This voice meant panic.

Alex grabbed me by my shoulders and looked me in the eyes. Instantly I calmed down a bit. "Okay. Let's think for a second," he said. "Are you sure you didn't bring one?"

"No! They said they'd have basic utensils and equipment, and we just needed to bring anything 'special.' I didn't think a broiler pan would be special." My voice had reached a new octave.

I eyed the other contestants setting out their ingredients

and utensils—*mise en place*, the French cooking term meaning roughly "everything in place." In my case, everything but a broiler pan. Why hadn't I read the list of provided equipment closer?

"What happens if you don't have a broiler pan . . . ? Not an option," Alex said, catching my expression. "Can you improvise?"

What was I going to do? Not having a broiler pan wouldn't ruin my dish, but it wouldn't be my best work. It wouldn't be Food TV–worthy. Crap Crapola Capital of Crapistan! I searched the room for some kind of answer.

"There!" I pointed at a girl two rows in front of me and three stations down. I knew it wasn't polite to point, but I didn't care. I exempted myself from caring. The girl was pulling a cooling rack used for baking from a drawer below the counter next to her oven. I yanked open my station's drawer and, as the heavens opened and angels sang, exhaled a sigh of relief. "It's not a broiler pan, but I can use this. I'll set it on a cookie sheet, and it'll let some of the fat drain from the meat as it cooks."

"That's disgusting," Alex said.

"Trust me. It's not."

Catastrophe averted. . . . So far, at least. I hadn't chopped one thing, hadn't even turned a knob on the oven, and already I was wondering what in the name of Bobby Flay I was doing there.

There was a moment I feared the cookie rack idea would be my downfall. Some fat from the lamb chops dripped onto the bottom of the oven and started to smoke. I had a vision of the hotel going up in flames. But the fat burned off, and the lamb came out perfect: crisp and brown on the outside, juicy on the inside, finger-lickin' good all over. Perched on top of a bed of fragrant white beans and spinach, these chops were the reason God created lambs. I was feeling good . . . until I saw other contestants' plates as they were whisked to the judges: a steaming dish of paella that released a saffron-scented cloud behind it, a silky chocolate mousse pie with a kiss of whipped cream that would have sent Martha Stewart into a fit of jealous rage. My confidence plummeted. I should have used more rosemary. Maybe I shouldn't have broiled at all and pan-seared. Did the beans have enough salt?

So I was shocked, shaken, stunned—almost traumatized—when the casting director climbed the stage and announced my name in the top ten. The shock quickly morphed into glee, which quickly dissolved into panic when I realized that meant I had to do an on-camera interview.

"Blew it," I said, collapsing into the chair next to Alex when I emerged from the interview room an hour and a half later.

"Are you sure?"

"Remember the time we had to make a video for history, and we pretended to be news anchors? But I kept forgetting my lines, and we'd have to start over again, so we decided I would just be the camerawoman, but then Mr. Marshall said I had to be in the video too, so we made me the weatherwoman, and everyone laughed because I mispronounced the word *meteorology* ten times?"

"Yeah."

"Worse. I don't even remember the questions. Something about my recipe, my goals, how I would describe myself. It was a blur. I babbled. I think I might have said something about Pappou's corns at one point."

Alex grimaced and leaned on his knees. "That bad, huh? Well, your lamb chops looked great."

"They were," I said glumly.

We sat in the lobby of the Marriott, staring at a painting that looked like splattered baby food for who knew how long, until I finally asked if we could just leave.

Alex pulled the earbud of the iPod we were sharing from his ear. "No, we cannot leave! You made it to the top ten!"

"Yeah, and that's as far as I'm going to make it. I don't see any reason to sit around and marinate—bad pun intended—in my humiliation. It's over, Alex."

I started to get up, but he stopped me. The Food TV woman had appeared from behind a closed door. Her clothes were wrinkled, and she looked tired. She smiled and addressed those of us who had hung around for their decision: the ten finalists, some friends and family, and a local newspaper reporter.

"You've been very patient," the woman said, tucking a strand of hair behind her ear. "Thank you for waiting. We are delighted to tell you that the winner of this qualifying competition for *Teen Test Kitchen* is . . ." The room was silent. I had the urge to grab Alex's hand, but I resisted. "Sophie Nicolaides with her rosemary lamb chops with white bean ragout." The woman navigated the foreign syllables of the name slowly. The name . . . it was my name!

"Shut up!" I yelled involuntarily. The woman looked

shocked. "Sorry," I apologized, realizing I was laughing like a lunatic. Everyone around me was clapping. "I can't believe it. Oh, my gosh."

Tommy Chang. I was going to meet Tommy Chang! And not only was I going to meet Tommy Chang, but I was going to take real culinary classes and compete for a scholarship and an internship in Tommy Chang's kitchen. Oh, my God . . . I was going to be on television.

"Congratulations," the Food TV woman said as she shook my hand. She put an arm around my shoulders as photographers snapped our picture. "We can't wait to have you in Napa."

And that's when it registered. Napa, as in California, as in that state on the opposite side of the country, for seven weeks. I'd never been away from home for more than a few days. Seven weeks away from my family and the restaurant and Alex . . . Whoa, I wanted to say all of a sudden, can I consider this first? But I was astonished at myself. What was I thinking? This was the chance of a lifetime, a chance I never thought I'd actually get. I really could be a famous chef. I repeated that to myself—I really could be a famous chef. Of course I would go on *Teen Test Kitchen*. But Alex couldn't forge this signature. I wasn't going anywhere if my father wouldn't let me.

"Dad." My voice was hesitant. Alex stood sheepishly behind me. I'd convinced him my father would not murder me with a witness in the room, though he could possibly murder us both.

The morning light slanted through the kitchen windows

onto the oilcloth-covered table where my father was enjoying the newspaper and a now-cold cup of sludgy Greek coffee. It was his Sunday morning tradition. He read the *Washington Post* from A1 to Obits, even the sections no one reads unless they're looking for something, like Real Estate and Jobs.

"Sophie . . . ," he said, mimicking my tentative tone. He laid the paper on the table and looked at me.

"What would you do if I told you I went to an audition yesterday?"

"I would say that's great. An audition for what?"

"What if I said a cooking competition, and I won?"

A smile lit his face. "That's excellent, Sophie! Why didn't you tell me about it?"

"What if I said the prize is to be on a reality TV show for teen chefs?" I held my breath for his response.

The skin between my father's caterpillarlike eyebrows crinkled. "Hold just a minute. I thought you were going to a football match yesterday." A shadow fell over his face. "What if we stop talking what-ifs, and you tell me what's going on?"

Alex slinked into the background by the refrigerator. "You can't be mad," I said.

"I most certainly can be mad," my father replied, his shoulders stiffening.

"Okay, well, try not to be. Because this is really exciting." I took a deep breath and sat at the table across from him. "I didn't go to a soccer game yesterday—and I'm sorry I lied to you. I went to an audition for a TV show, a cooking show, but I didn't want to get your hopes up in case I didn't win. I never thought I'd win—but I did! Dad, I won!"

"And what did you win, Sophia?"

Sophia, not Sophie. This meant he was not pleased, not pleased at all. Only my grandparents called me Sophia—the name meant "wisdom," which seemed not very suitable at the moment. I'd lied to my father and forged his name on a permission form. The scheme sounded less and less "wise" by the moment.

"I won a spot on a TV show where teen chefs compete for a scholarship and an apprenticeship with one of the greatest chefs in the world."

My father did not seem as impressed by this explanation as I had hoped, even with the word *scholarship* strategically emphasized.

"A TV show?" He raised one bushy eyebrow. "And why would I want my sixteen-year-old daughter to be on a reality TV show?"

"Because it's a once-in-a-lifetime opportunity?" I slanted the words upward hopefully.

"And where is this TV show going to be filmed, may I ask? I assume it is not in Fairfax, Virginia."

"At the National Culinary Academy. It's the best culinary school in the country, Dad. . . . It's in California."

"California?" He half roared, half laughed. "Hollywood?"

"No, Napa Valley."

Some unrecognizable expression flickered across his face. "And how long would you be spending in California?" His accent came out thick as he said it: Cal-ee-forn-ee-a.

"Seven weeks." Admittedly, it sounded like a long time to me as well.

"Absolutely not. I need you at the restaurant." He picked

up his newspaper, snapping its pages to attention. The patriarch had spoken.

"But, Dad—" I started.

"Mr. Nicolaides, I'm sure I can cover Sophie's shifts at the restaur—" My father gave Alex a look that said, Butt out or I will kick your butt out. "All righty, then! I'll be in the den." Alex made a hasty exit just as Raffi came into the kitchen.

"But, Dad," I tried again.

"No *buts*," Raffi said, parroting one of our father's favorite Americanisms. He stuck his head into the refrigerator and rooted around a bit. I wanted to shut him in. "What are you *but*-ing about anyway?"

"I won a contest."

"A contest for dorks who are in love with their only friend?"

I glared at him and prayed that Alex couldn't hear in the other room, where Nonna was watching the Home Shopping Network on high volume. "No," I said. "A contest for teen chefs. It's going to be on TV."

"Like public access? Awesome. You and the rapping rabbi." Raffi was referring to a local public television show we liked to make fun of.

"No, on national television. On Food TV."

My father remained silent, as if this conversation wasn't going on around him.

Raffi lowered the orange juice container from his mouth. He had my father's dark hair and olive skin but my mother's blue eyes, which reconsidered me now. "Wait. You really won a contest to be on TV?"

"It's a reality show where teen chefs take classes at the National Culinary Academy and compete for a scholarship"—I emphasized the word again, in case my dad missed it the first time—"and an apprenticeship with Tommy Chang. You probably don't know who he is, but he's like the biggest—"

"Celebrity chef in America? Yeah, I'm not some food nerd like you, but I'm not living in a cave, Sophie. So are you gonna do it?" If I hadn't known better, I'd have said Raffi actually sounded excited.

I looked at my father.

"No," he answered for me, his gaze not veering from his paper. "She is not going to do it."

Raffi's eyes widened. "O-kay," he mouthed to me.

Time to switch tactics. "Dad—Baba," I said, using the Greek word for "dad," not above exploiting his sentimentality. "This is an amazing opportunity. Think about how much I'll learn. Aunt Mary's out there. And it would be good for Taverna Ristorante—"

"No, Sophia."

"But, Dad." My voice was beseeching now, almost pathetic.

"No, Sophia."

Tears stung my eyes. I'd never thought I'd make it on the show, but I had. I'd beaten fifty-six other chefs! Maybe I *was* good enough for this thing. Maybe this was my Golden Ticket. And now my father was going to take it all away from me. Did he want to keep me at Taverna Ristorante forever?

"I'll run away, you know." I hadn't threatened to run away since I was ten, and I was embarrassed even as I said it.

My father was silent.

"I can't believe you!" I shouted. I never shouted at my father. Never. I didn't even know how he'd react to yelling. He sat as quiet and stony as a statue.

"Fine," I said.

He turned to the Metro section.

When my father's mind was made up, there was only one person capable of changing it—Nonna.

"Can you hear what they're saying?" Alex whispered.

I put my finger to my lips and shook my head. Alex pressed his ear next to mine against the thin door to my grandparents' room. We could hear urgent voices inside, but they were in Italian. Without subtitles, we could understand about as much as "Napa," "Sophia," "*figlia*" (daughter), and another name Alex didn't recognize, "Maria."

"Who's Maria?" he mouthed.

"My aunt Mary. The one who lives in Napa."

Footsteps fell heavily toward the door, and we bolted to the den, throwing ourselves on the couch. My father entered, his face flushed from what was apparently a vigorous conversation.

"Sophia?" he said.

"Yes?"

"May I talk to you in the kitchen?"

I tossed the garden catalog I'd been pretending to read onto the coffee table, shared a nervous look with Alex, and followed my father out of the room.

He stood in front of the sink, lips pursed and arms crossed

over his wide chest. He was not happy about what he was about to say. He inhaled deeply. "Despite the fact that I am very disappointed you lied to me yesterday—"

I started to interject, but he held up a hand to say, Don't press your luck. "I have decided that I will let you participate in the show."

I flew across the linoleum and threw my arms around his neck. "On the condition," he continued pointedly, "that I am satisfied it is a good educational opportunity and not some free-for-all, hormones-gone-wild spring-break party."

"Dad, it's a good show. It's really a good show. I think they really want to find good chefs." *Really* and *good* were as articulate as I could be at that moment.

There was more. "While you're there," he said, "I think you should see your mother's sister if you can."

"Aunt Mary?"

"It would be good for you to spend some time with your mother's family," my father said. "And if anything goes wrong, she can—"

"Nothing will go wrong!" I kissed both cheeks. "Thank you, Dad. Alex!" I rushed into the den with the good news. My tiny but all-powerful grandmother was sitting on the couch next to him. They both looked up, and Alex grinned.

"Thank you, Nonna," I said.

She took my hands in her soft, wrinkly ones and winked. "You win the gold, *nipotina*," she said in her lilting English. "You make the Nicolaides proud."

"I will. I'll try," I corrected, myself.

"I wish you could come with me," I said to Alex, feeling suddenly vulnerable as I did.

"Nah." He tossed his bangs out of his eyes. "I'd just be in your way. Just promise not to forget the little people once you're a big reality TV star."

I laughed. "Trust me, there is nothing real about this."

Rosemary Lamb Chops with Spinach and White Bean Ragout

The dish that started it all. (Drumroll, please.) You can make the lamb using your oven's broiler (don't forget the broiler pan—or a cooling rack over a cookie sheet works in a pinch), or on a grill. Simmer the spinach and white beans for about 15 minutes to let the flavors develop; you can keep the ragout warm for up to an hour. If it starts to look dry (happens to the best of us), just add a little more stock.

SERVES 4

Ingredients

For the Spinach and White Bean Ragout

2 (15-ounce) cans white beans (like cannellini or Great Northern), drained
1/2 cup chicken stock
3 fresh rosemary sprigs
1 clove garlic, minced
3 cups baby spinach leaves
Kosher salt and freshly ground black pepper to taste

For the Rosemary Lamb Chops

12 lamb rib chops (the small ones, about 1 inch thick)
1/2 cup extra-virgin olive oil
4 cloves garlic, minced

$^1/_4$ cup fresh rosemary leaves, minced
Kosher salt and freshly ground black pepper to taste

Directions

1. For the ragout, combine beans, stock, rosemary, garlic, spinach, salt, and pepper in a small pot over low heat. Simmer while you prepare the lamb chops.

2. Preheat the broiler on your oven. Rub lamb chops with olive oil, then sprinkle both sides with garlic, rosemary, salt, and pepper. Broil the chops 4 to 5 inches from heat, for about $3^1/_2$ minutes (longer if they're thicker, shorter if they're thinner). Flip the chops over and broil on other side for $3^1/_2$ minutes. Remove chops from broiler and let rest for 3 to 5 minutes.

3. Spoon the spinach and white bean ragout onto each plate, and top with the lamb chops.

Chapter Three

My ears wouldn't pop. I hated flying. I'd imagined a private Food TV jet whisking me away from Dulles International Airport with a smoothie in my hand and a cashmere blanket thrown over my knees. Instead, I was sandwiched in coach between a woman juggling a squirming toddler on her lap and a man whose grease-spotted bag of fast food was making me feel sick to my stomach. The polyester seat was scratchy on my legs and kind of grossing me out. So much for my new jet-set lifestyle.

I closed my eyes and tried to breathe deeply, but French Fry Man next to me was making that difficult. Instead I thought about Alex, or more precisely about our very anticlimactic good-bye at the airport. He'd come with Raffi and my father to drop me off.

Over the past month, I'd tried to drop casual hints that

being away from him for seven weeks was really gonna suck. The rules in the thick information packet the producers sent me were very clear that contestants' communication with the outside world would be limited and closely monitored. There would be no cell phones, no e-mailing, no texting back home. We got two calls a week to our parents, like prison. It made me nervous to think of going that long without talking to Alex. The longest we'd been without speaking was a week in eighth grade, when the Underhills took a vacation to Costa Rica. What if he forgot about me? What if Lindy moved in? I had inserted a few well-placed disses in our recent conversations just to make sure Alex knew she was not a suitable substitute for my company while I was gone.

I wasn't quite sure what I was expecting our good-bye at the airport to look like—flowers, proclamations, tears? Whatever I got definitely wasn't it: a clap on the back and an order to kick some top-chef tail. About as much emotion as he'd show his little brother leaving for Boy Scout camp.

The baby on the plane next to me started to squeal, and I decided I needed an attitude adjustment. I was embarking on an adventure, a terrifying and amazing adventure. So what if I came back to Alex and Lindy dating (though the thought did make me want to vomit)? I'd come back a celebrity chef. And that was what was important.

My resolution to face forward, not back, led me to a recurring daydream. I was on a red carpet, but not just any red carpet. This was the red carpet at the opening of my future restaurant. I'd already decided on a name: Sophie. It had a nice ring to it. The paparazzi were there, and celebrities: Martha Stewart and Rachael Ray, Robert Pattinson, Brad, Angelina and Jennifer, Drew, of course. Reporters jostled each other for my attention. "Sophie!" they yelled. "Sophie! Just one question: How does it feel to be the youngest chef ever awarded three Michelin stars?" My honest but appropriately modest answer: "It feels great."

At some point I wasn't daydreaming anymore; I was real dreaming, because I woke to the bump of the plane's wheels on the tarmac. I closed my mouth, which apparently had been hanging open for some time, and tried to orient myself as I stared out the window. A sign welcomed me to San Francisco International Airport. There was no turning back now.

The limo swung around a bend in the road, and I saw it—the National Culinary Academy. It rose up out of the lush, green vineyards of Napa Valley like the Emerald City in *The Wizard of Oz*. I wanted to sing "Over the Rainbow." I wanted to frolic through a field of poppies with Toto and the Tin Man. I could not believe I was in this beautiful place.

I'd spent at least two hundred hours leading up to this moment poring over the NCA website and brochures the producers sent. I even kept one tucked beneath my pillow, as if the culinary fairy might pay a visit and wave her magic wand, granting me supernatural cooking powers. Still, the NCA building was even grander than the glossy catalogs suggested. It looked more like a castle or a cathedral than a school. The gray stone building had soaring spires and huge windows that glittered against the blue, cloudless sky. I halfway expected to see a moat as we drove closer.

The limo pulled between two hulking iron gates that framed the entrance and proceeded up the driveway. I counted seven stretch limos already lined up in front of the building—and a circus of cameramen, sound people, producers, and assistants scurrying to greet them. The euphoria receded, and suddenly I didn't just have butterflies; I had giant luna moths dive-bombing around my stomach, flapping their wings double time.

Pulling back from the window, I stared straight ahead at the license plate on the limo in front of me. I gnawed unconsciously at a stubby fingernail. "Sophie," my dad always said, "why must you eat your fingernails when we have such a beautiful meal right here in front of us?" I realized the cameraman sitting opposite me in the back of my limo was zooming in on my fingernail snack, and I quickly extracted my hand from my mouth, shoving it under my leg.

One by one, the limos were delivering their contestants onto a red carpet rolled out on a ramp laid over the NCA's wide stone stairs. I craned my neck to see if I could catch a glimpse of the other chefs, but as soon as the limo doors opened, they were swarmed by people. All I saw was a suitcase here, a Converse-clad foot there, a shock of red hair above the fray. I wondered if my limo being last meant anything. It crept to the drop-off point.

"You ready?" the cameraman asked. His voice was gruff, but he smiled from behind his lens. I was a little taken off guard, as those were the first words he'd spoken since I was greeted by a production assistant in San Francisco. I thought the cameramen weren't allowed to talk to us. In the show guidelines, we were instructed to think of them as our "shadows."

"Ready as I'll ever be," I murmured to myself as much as to him.

The limo stopped, and my door swung open. A thicket of cameras and microphones bore down on me.

Anticipating this very moment, Alex had forwarded me a series of paparazzi shots of several overexposed starlets incorrectly exiting their vehicles, with the subject line DON'T BE THIS GIRL. His idea of a joke, but now I concentrated hard on getting out of the limo without revealing my unmentionables.

My feet touched red, and a man dressed in all black and wearing headphones was in front of me in a flash. The cameras lowered and sound guys fiddled with mics as the man introduced himself in an Australian accent.

"Hello, Sophie." He extended his hand, and I shook it, wondering if the man's pumpkiny shade of tan would rub off on me. He wore a baseball cap under his headphones. "My name is Peter Martin. I'm the field producer for *Teen Test Kitchen*. Welcome to Napa."

"Thanks." I had no idea what a field producer was. I wondered where the nice woman from the Marriott was. I liked her. This guy, on the other hand, made me uneasy.

Everyone else milling around the NCA entrance seemed perfectly at ease, just going about their jobs, checking light readings, fiddling with equipment, running cables like any other day, business as usual, la-di-da. But I was overwhelmed. I jumped when a young woman swooped in to check the wireless microphone that had been clipped to my skirt waist at the airport.

"Sorry," I said.

"Testing, testing," the woman said. Then, giving the thumbs-up to someone, "We're good!" She moved on without acknowledging me.

Peter smiled. He had disturbingly white teeth. "So we're gonna pick up right where we left off, okay?" He made eye contact with a cameraman and nodded at me enthusiastically as he spoke, like you'd talk to a kindergartner. "You just keep going into the building and up the elevator to the kitchen. You're the last one in, so the other contestants are already there. And remember, don't look into the cameras."

I nodded. So a field producer was like a director. Who knew reality needed directing?

"Great!" Peter flashed another smile and stepped off the red carpet into the throng of people. "Action," he yelled.

I froze. What did the man just tell me to do? Someone began wildly waving her arms and gesturing for me to continue up the red carpet and through the double doors. I thought I was moving forward, but as I took a step, my shoulder jerked back, and I nearly fell. The wheel on my suitcase was stuck on the edge of the carpet. I dislodged it and turned—*smack!*—into a long pole just inches from my face.

"Watch the boom," someone said one second too late.

"Thanks." I grimaced, rubbing my forehead.

"Cut!" the field producer/director yelled. "Are you okay?" he asked, rushing toward me.

"Yeah." The only thing injured was my pride.

"You're sure? You don't need ice or anything?"

"No, I'm fine."

"Okay. We're gonna start again. Just up the ramp and into the building."

"Right." I nodded.

"Action!" he yelled again.

Above the oversize brass and wood doors of the National Culinary Academy's entrance, a quotation was etched in the stone.

A GOOD COOK IS THE PECULIAR GIFT OF THE GODS
—WALTER SAVAGE LANDOR

No truer words were ever written, I thought and smiled. Finally, I had arrived.

Inside the doors, a cavernous atrium echoed with the clinking and tinkling of the kitchens two and three floors above. The familiar sound was comforting. My eyes wandered over portraits of the famous NCA graduates who once walked these hallowed halls and now ran five-star restaurants, hosted hit food shows, and baked for presidents and Oprah. They decorated the lobby like championship pennants decorated my school gym. Could this be a dream?

A couple of regular NCA students in white chef's jackets hurried past me. It felt rehearsed, like they'd been released from a cage and directed across the room in front of me. I had to smile, though, at their toques. Of course I'd seen the traditional hats before, but mostly on TV and in movies, never in a real kitchen. The closest we got to toques at Taverna Ristorante were backward baseball caps and bandannas.

A camera crew shadowed me, their long black cables coiling and uncoiling like tails behind them, to the elevator. It opened and I stepped in, and was surprised when they didn't follow. The doors pinged closed, and for the first time since I got off the plane, I was alone. Squinching my eyes shut, I did my spastic happy dance, the one where I ball my fists and shake them like maracas. Only when I opened them again did I realize why the cameras didn't have to follow me into the elevator: its sides were made of glass. The cameras were panning from the floor below. So much for playing it cool.

When the elevator doors opened again, I was greeted by yet another camera and crew. Across from me was a door emblazoned with the show's logo: the words *Teen* and *Test Kitchen* sliced through by a rather menacing knife. The door was closing on a very tall, very thin brunette pulling a roller suitcase. I followed.

In the kitchen there was too much to take in at once. It was information overload. The room was brightly lit, and there seemed to be cameras in every corner. Stadium-style seating allowed maximum viewing of the spotless stainless-steel kitchen at the front of the room. In the seats sat my competition. Some of them were still evaluating the girl who'd come in ahead of me. She snapped the handle down on her roller bag and claimed a seat, folding her hands neatly on the desk in front of her. Others had turned their gazes on me.

There was a wispy Asian boy wearing trendy thick-rimmed glasses. He was staring at the brunette. Next to him was another boy, Hispanic, who looked, strangely, bored.

The redhead I'd glimpsed on the red carpet was next to him. Whispering with her was a blond Barbie of a girl. She reminded me of a certain cheerleader at school as she twisted a golden lock of hair around her finger. A row back sat a cute African-American guy with short, spiky braids. His eyes were glued to the desk in front of him. In the very front row, a well-fed boy in a bright pink polo shirt chatted excitedly with the brunette, who'd just sat next to him. Four girls, four boys, all the colors of the rainbow. I sat on the other side of the pudgy prepster, who was making no effort to keep his voice down.

"Stanley Goldberg," he said immediately, sticking out his hand for a shake. "But you can call me Stan. Or Derek. I much prefer that to Stan any day. It's an awful, awful, soul-killing kind of name to give a kid, don't you think? Don't worry, you don't have to answer that."

Stanley—Stan—was talking in such an uninterrupted stream of words, I could barely make out what he was saying.

"I'm from New York—Manhattan," he continued, undeterred by the blank look on my face. "Like you can call anything else New York. I mean, if you're from Brooklyn, you should say Brooklyn." He clapped his hand over his mouth. "Sorry. That sounded awful, didn't it? My parents told me to try not to sound like a snob. It might be off-putting to the judges. What's your name?"

The brunette was watching me now too. I realized it was my turn to speak. "Sophie," I answered. "Nicolaides."

"Ooh, I like that," Stan said, making his eyes look dreamy. "Nicolaides. Are you Greek?"

"Greek-Italian. My grandmother's Italian, and my grandfather's Greek."

Stan's eyes widened. "Oh, how fun! Don't you just love Mykonos? Oh, and Tuscany! I felt like I'd died and gone to carb heaven. Of course, not like here. I mean this"—Stan held his hands out and palm-up to take in the kitchen, the school, Napa—"this is Mecca. Am I right?"

I laughed. "You're right."

"I know! It's crazy, right?"

I opened my mouth to respond but saw Stan's attention dart to some point behind my head. He sat up straighter, and it was suddenly as if all the air in the room had been sucked out. I turned to see what everyone was looking at: The judges had arrived.

One by one, they filed in and stood behind the kitchen's prep table. They gazed up at us, looking like either executioners or guardian angels. There were four in all, and I was happy that I recognized three of them. From left to right, they were François Bouchard, the head chef at the NCA for the past eight years and a master of French cuisine with two Michelin stars to his name; Patricia Hooks, founder and editor-in-chief of *Foodie* magazine at only thirty years old; and, of course, Tommy Chang, who exuded the same sense of Zen self-assurance that he always exhibited on TV. The last man I didn't recognize. He was short, very lean, and bald, with sharp features and glasses perched on a beaklike nose. He wore a pinched expression and looked like he might suddenly yell something in German. Was I supposed to know who he was? I stole a sideways glance to see if my fellow chefs seemed to have a clue, but I couldn't tell.

The judges let what felt like an eternity of suspense-building silence pass before Tommy finally stepped forward and spoke.

"Welcome, chefs, to *Teen Test Kitchen*." There was something almost ominous in his voice. "Over the next seven weeks, you will experience what it's like to be a student at the prestigious National Culinary Academy in Napa Valley. You will be trained by world-class chefs in this state-of-the-art facility." Pause so the cameras could scan the tricked-out kitchen. "Each week, you will have a chance to show the judges what you've learned. And each week, one chef will be at the top of the class. In the end, only three of you will return for the finale to compete for a scholarship to the NCA and a one-month apprenticeship at my flagship restaurant, Om, in New York City."

The feeling in the room was electric. This was it. This was real.

"So, chefs, sharpen your knives. Because there will be a test."

I had a feeling we would be hearing that line again.

Tommy Chang's Spicy Korean Chicken Lollipops

I'll admit, the first time I heard the words *chicken* and *lollipop* in the same sentence, I gagged. But this is one of Tommy Chang's signature dishes, and trust me when I say it's droolworthy. They're called "lollipops" because you push all the meat on the drumette to the top, so it looks like . . . well . . . a chicken lollipop. The sauce is the perfect mix of salty, sweet, and the savory flavor the Japanese call *umami*. Alex likes me to dash in some hot sauce, too. Note: Frying can be dangerous (witness the burn on my hand), so this recipe is best tried by experienced cooks. Never leave hot oil unattended, and never let another liquid (like a glass of water or a drink) spill into the oil.

SERVES 4

Ingredients

2 tablespoons sugar
1 clove garlic, minced
1/2 teaspoon freshly ground black pepper
1/2 cup soy sauce
1/2 cup hoisin sauce
2 tablespoons honey
1 teaspoon sesame oil
hot sauce (optional)

Canola or vegetable oil, for frying
3 1/2 pounds chicken drumettes
Kosher salt
All-purpose flour, for dusting
1 tablespoon toasted sesame seeds, for garnish
4 sliced scallions, for garnish

Directions

1. In a medium saucepan, combine sugar, garlic, soy sauce, hoisin, honey, sesame oil, black pepper, and hot sauce (if you're using it) over low heat.

2. Preheat oven to 400°F. In a deep pot, slowly bring 3 inches of oil to 325°F. (You can test the temperature by dropping a cube of bread in the oil; if it toasts, you have the right temperature. Don't let the oil get so hot that it smokes!)

3. While the oven and pot are heating, shape the chicken drumettes. With a sharp paring knife, carefully cut through the skin and any sinew surrounding the bone at the small end of the drumette. Hold it firmly by that end and scrape the meat and skin to the top of the bone. Use your fingers to pull the meat over so it's inside out (it'll look like a ball on a stick). Season the chicken with salt and pepper and dust generously with flour. Set a metal rack over a rimmed cookie sheet near the

stove. Working in batches, fry the drumettes (careful when you drop them in—I use tongs) until browned and crisp, about 8 minutes. Drain the drumettes on the rack and keep warm in the oven while frying the rest.

4. Hold each fried drumette by the "stick" end and dunk it into the warm barbecue sauce, then place on a platter. Sprinkle with sesame seeds and scallions and serve with plenty of napkins. (Remember, used cooking oil never goes down the sink drain. Learned that the hard way! I pour mine into a glass jar I keep in the freezer. Somewhat gross but less messy.)

Week 1

THE BASICS

Chapter Four

You couldn't really call the NCA dining room a cafeteria. It wasn't like any cafeteria I'd ever seen. There wasn't the whiff of institutional oppression of my past three school cafeterias. It looked more like an enormous modern restaurant, with high, vaulted ceilings, white linens on the tables, and real flowers in glass vases, not the plastic ones that have to be dusted periodically.

Students developed the menu and ran food service from a series of buffet lines. There was even a sushi station and sometimes a raw bar, both stocked from the Pacific, which lapped the shore just fifty miles west. I supposed one of the top culinary institutions in the world couldn't very well serve fish sticks.

A production assistant, or assistant producer—I was having a hard time figuring out who did what—had showed us around campus, including the dorms where we'd be staying, and then deposited us at the cafeteria in time for dinner, where Peter, or the MIB (short for Man in Black, as Stan had already taken to calling him behind his back), was waiting for us.

The cameras orbited as Shelby, the tall brunette—and my new roommate—and I got our food and joined the table. "How about we play a little get-to-know-each-other game?" the MIB said cheerily. I stifled a groan, thinking of my summers at YMCA camp. Shelby must have had similar associations, because I noticed she rolled her eyes. "We'll go around the table, and you tell us where you're from, how old you are, how you got into cooking, and your favorite dish. And, remember, no last names on camera. Mario, you start."

Mario looked as if he'd just been called "goose" in a game of Duck, Duck, Goose. He cleared his throat.

"Uh, I'm Mario. I'm sixteen years old, and I'm from San Antonio, Texas. My family owns a restaurant—that's where I learned to cook." Just like me, I thought. "We also just launched a line of salsas," he added proudly. "Salsa Mamacita. And my favorite dish is beef barbacoa."

When prompted by Peter, Mario took great pleasure in describing how, to be authentic, barbacoa had to be made with a cow head. Maura, the fifteen-year-old redhead from Boston, looked like she might lose her dinner. She had been vegetarian until last year, surely a disadvantage, which I silently noted. She started baking with her grandmother and liked potato gratin with Gruyère cheese.

Britney was the oldest at almost eighteen, from somewhere in Southern California. She liked lasagna, which sounded unoriginal, but I couldn't blame her. The low-cut pink tank top she was wearing was not exactly kitchen-ready but certainly accentuated her . . . perkiness. She got on the show somehow, though, so I knew I shouldn't discount her. Dante was only fifteen, although he looked much older. He was from Atlanta and also learned to cook from his grandmother. I expected him to say his favorite dish was something sinfully Southern, worthy of a "Paula Deen Y'all." So he surprised me when he said he liked curry—another competitor not to be underestimated.

We continued around the table. Philip was sixteen. He was born in South Korea but moved to San Francisco when he was six. His father taught him to cook, and his favorite dish was Thai lemongrass beef. Stan, as everyone knew by now, was from New York City. "Park Avenue," he clarified, which elicited a *pfft* from Mario. He learned to make his favorite dish, Oysters Rockefeller, from his family's chef. If some kids were born with a silver spoon in their mouths, it seemed Stan was born with a platinum ladle. Shelby was seventeen. She was from Benton, Wisconsin, and clearly not thrilled about that fact. She taught herself to bake and cook, including her favorite dish, salmon in mustard sauce with rice pilaf.

And we had arrived at me. Sophie, DC, an Easy-Bake Oven, a *real* Greek salad—no lettuce, with large hunks of creamy feta and black Kalamata olives.

"Your family has a Greek restaurant?" asked Peter.

"Greek-Italian," I corrected him.

Seven sets of eyes sized me up. Friend or foe, they wondered. I knew because I was thinking the same thing about them.

The restaurant was the first thing the MIB revisited later that night in my Kitchen Confidential video diary. Throughout the show, we'd be asked to sit in a glorified coat closet and answer the MIB's questions in front of a camera.

"Tell me, Sophie," he asked, sounding not unlike Russell Crowe as he cupped his chin in his hand and balanced a clipboard on his knee, "do you think of yourself primarily as a Mediterranean chef?"

I was having trouble concentrating, knowing that whatever I said in these interviews would be public record, spliced into a billion pieces and shot through fiber-optic wires to America's living rooms. The MIB was staring at me unblinkingly. It was unnerving, actually, how little he felt the need to blink.

"No," I answered carefully. "I mean, my family is from the Mediterranean, but I don't want to be a Mediterranean chef . . . to be *just* a Mediterranean chef," I corrected. "I want to cook all kinds of foods."

My neck and cheeks felt suddenly warm. I wasn't used to talking to the camera. All day they kept telling us not to look at them. Now the MIB silently directed my gaze to the lens. I stumbled through the rest of his questions, about how I felt when I first arrived at the NCA—was it really just that morning?—and if I was intimidated by the judges. That last question felt like bait. If I was intimidated by the blank, glassy eye of a camera lens, how did he think I felt in front of a panel of culinary superstars who had my hopes and dreams on a chopping block? The worst, though, was Stefan Ziegler.

Stefan, the trim bald man I hadn't recognized that

morning, had been introduced as Tommy's executive sous-chef at Om. I had seen pictures of Om once in a copy of *Travel+Leisure* at the doctor's office. It wasn't just a restaurant; it was a French-Brazilian-Asian fusion temple to food. A giant Buddha head loomed over fabulously dressed diners. Through the middle of the enormous dining room, a stream of clear water trickled over white pebbles, eventually cascading into a koi pond by the bar. In the photo, the kitchen was a blur of color, open to it all like a sideshow. The article said Tommy's restaurant in Hong Kong was even more extravagant, with live peacocks roaming the patio. I couldn't place the dour, pinched little man Tommy introduced as Stefan Ziegler at a restaurant like that. But whether I liked him or not, Stefan would be the show's de facto host in Tommy's absence, and our custodian.

After meeting us in the Test Kitchen, Tommy, Chef Bouchard, and Patricia left. But Stefan stayed to explain how the next seven weeks would unfold. He paced the front of the room, his fingers steepled condescendingly in front of him and the lights bouncing off his bald head. His words were sharp and clipped, as if he didn't want to waste them. Each week we would focus on the flavors and techniques of a different region's cuisine. There would be classes in the mornings and cooking labs in the afternoons, where we would try what had been demonstrated that morning. Every Friday, we would have a test on what we had learned. The dishes we prepared would be graded on three elements: technique, judged by Chef Bouchard; flavor, judged by Patricia; and visual appeal, judged by Tommy. Each week, we "started from scratch," meaning the previous week's winner had no better chance of being at the "top of the class" than any other chef. The three chefs at the top of the seventh week would compete in the live finale in November. The focus of our first week, rather than a specific cuisine, would be the basics, starting with knife skills.

While Stefan talked, a cloud of disappointment settled over the kitchen as we realized we wouldn't be hanging out with Tommy Chang. We would be hanging out with this guy. Tommy Chang was just garnish.

"So," Stefan barked at the end of our orientation, "are there any questions?" No one had been brave enough to raise a hand.

The air in Napa was different than in DC. It was warm but dry, which made the lush green valley that spread out around the NCA seem like a mirage. But the night was cool and clear. A million stars blanketed the sky. Behind our dorm there was a stone patio dotted with wrought-iron tables and chairs. Shelby and I decided to take up residence there. Stan joined us and right away offered some much-needed comic relief from the stressful day. His impersonation of Stefan was spot-on.

"So!" He held himself taut and snapped a stick he had found on the ground on his leg like a riding crop. "Are there any questions?"

I laughed, but cautiously. Stan was brave. After eight P.M., we were allowed to take off our mic packs, but there was still the unsettling feeling that the place was more bugged than a Russian embassy. Who knew where cameras or more mics might be hidden—in a potted plant, on a lamppost, on a person? The fact that I couldn't see any cameras only made me more wary of their presence.

"You know he graduated from the NCA?" said Shelby, meaning Stefan.

"Is that so?" Stan said. Unimpressed, he plucked up a leaf that had tumbled onto his neatly pressed khakis.

I'd decided I liked Shelby. Already I could tell she was the kind of person who said what she meant and meant what she said. No crap, and there was a wicked sense of humor in there somewhere. Her long legs were folded under her in her chair, but she had to be six feet tall, and she was extremely skinny. She reminded me of a praying mantis, or a walking stick. I always got those two insects confused.

She was chewing on the ends of her chestnut-colored hair. "Yeah. He's been working for Tommy for, like, fifteen years now. Talk about being somebody's biyatch. I think I'd want my own restaurant by then."

I nodded noncommittally, unable to shake the feeling that Stefan and Tommy were listening to us somewhere.

"No kidding," Stan snorted. His legs were crossed, revealing a pale stripe of plump ankle above a pair of expensive-looking loafers. I'd decided I liked him too.

The rest of the "cheftestants," as they were calling us, were already in bed or hanging out in the dorm's commons room, which was decorated with brightly colored modern furniture and food-themed pop art obviously brought in for the show. I wondered if we should be in there socializing with them.

Dante seemed nice but was quiet. Maura had a strange

way of staring off into space, and Britney hadn't said anything particularly intelligent since we'd gotten there, but I supposed I hadn't either. I was too busy taking in my surroundings—and my competition. For no reason I could put my finger on, Philip and Mario were the players I wasn't sure I could trust.

My voice dropped to a whisper. "What do you guys think of the others?"

"I'm not concerned," Shelby replied at usual volume. "I Googled everyone before I got here." She reconsidered. "Except maybe Philip. He looks good."

"I'd love to have been a fly on the wall at that casting meeting," said Stan.

"What do you mean?" I asked.

Stan raised one eyebrow. "Please. Can't you see the producers checking off their little boxes?" He pretended to make checkmarks on an imaginary list on his palm. "Petite? Check. Asian? Check. Overachiever with potential authority issues? Check. It's not a reality cooking show till you've got one."

"So you don't think he's good enough to be here?" Shelby asked.

"That's not what I said."

I was shocked by Stan's politically incorrect bluntness. You weren't supposed to talk like that, especially not when you were on television. My surprise must have been written on my face because Stan continued. "Look at all of us! We're like the United Colors of Benetton. A smorgasbord of diversity! You think that was unintentional?"

My heart sank a little as Shelby laughed in agreement.

Sure, I'd noticed the same rainbow effect when I'd walked into the kitchen that morning, but what if I wanted to believe I'd gotten there on merit rather than stereotyping?

"Who would you be then?" Shelby asked Stan. Her knees were tucked under her chin. Now she reminded me of a bird, not an insect at all. She was pretty, I thought.

Stan lit up, his hands splayed across his chest. "Gay? Check. Fat? Check. Pushy New Yorker. Check."

"You're not fat," I said, although the boyish roundness of Stan's face and the belly that stretched his polo shirt confirmed otherwise.

"I'm just glad to have the market cornered." He winked, clasping his hands coquettishly around his crossed knees. I had to wonder if he was always this camp, or if he was playing it up for the cameras. Wherever they were.

"Let's see," said Shelby. She dropped the chewed ends of her hair from her mouth and pursed her lips. "Skinny? Check. Bitch? Check. From Podunk, Wisconsin. Not sure that would be on anyone's checklist." She smiled, pleased with her less-than-complimentary, but admittedly spot-on, self-stereotype. "And in what role were you cast, Sophie?"

I hadn't thought of it that way. At least talking about it made it funny instead of insulting. "Motherless Mediterranean misfit?" I offered.

Stan laughed, then quickly overcorrected with a frown. "I mean, I'm sorry about the motherless part."

"Thanks, but it was a long time ago." I was used to delivering this line. People got so weird when they found out your mother had died. But they only got weirder when you told them you never knew her.

"So why are you really here?" Stan wiggled his expressive eyebrows.

The wind rustled the leaves of the vineyards behind us. It was a comforting white noise, like waves crashing on a beach.

Shelby answered first. "I want to win so I can get the hell out of Wisconsin," she said matter-of-factly. "Plus it would really piss off my older sister."

"Fair enough." Stan turned an expectant gaze on me. I paused a second to form my words better than I had in my Kitchen Confidential.

"I want to do something more with my life than run my family's restaurant. I want my own restaurant, a really good one that people talk about and write about." Yep, that sounded about right. "What about you?"

Stan heaved a dramatic sigh. "Tale as old as time. I want to show my parents that I'm more than a trust-fund baby. That, and my horoscope said I have all the ingredients for success this moon phase if I just apply myself and remember to taste, taste, taste."

"Your horoscope told you that?"

"In so many words."

Shelby stood and stretched. How could a chef be so skinny? "Well, kids, it's written in *my* stars that I have to get to bed."

Stan and I stood to go also, but something Shelby had said earlier stuck in my head. "Did you say you Googled everybody before you got here? I didn't even think to do that. How did you know who the other contestants were?"

Shelby rubbed her arms over her long-sleeved T-shirt

and yawned. "I did a news search for all the casting competitions. Most local newspapers covered it. I kept a notebook with what I was able to find on everyone, but the producers took it when I got here."

"They took my diary," Stan grumbled. "A boy needs to journal through his stress, ya know."

Our sixty-six-page contract had clearly stated that we could not bring any cookbooks, recipes, or other cooking-related literature to the competition. We would all be provided with the same instruction during our time on the show, and any outside materials would be seen as an unfair advantage. It hadn't said that we would have all booklike things taken from us.

I thought of the Moleskine journal Alex had given me two years ago that was now locked away in some producer's office and experienced a sharp pang of homesickness. I wondered what Alex was doing at that moment. Where was he? It was three hours later there. Maybe he was at the ninety-nine-cent movie theater we liked, or at the mall. But more important, who was he with? I only hoped it wasn't Lindy.

I stood in front of the shiny steel table, bleary-eyed. I was pretty sure there was still a crease from my pillow running the length of my cheek. If it weren't for the ridiculously beautiful scene outside my window and the adrenaline rush of our first day in the kitchen, I would have delivered a volley of choice words to the production assistant who rapped her knuckles on my door at six A.M. Best case scenario, I had slept four hours. I had turned the blaring red numbers of my alarm clock away from me when they threatened 2:17 A.M.

Stefan stared at us over his nose. "Good morning, chefs," he said briskly.

"Good morning," we chimed in unison, dutifully ignoring the three cameras and six crew members in our peripheral vision.

"Good morning, *Chef.* That is how you will address me," he snapped.

In front of Stefan was a large wooden cutting board. A black canvas knife roll was unfurled across the table. Twelve knives and utensils of varying shapes and sizes gleamed from its pockets. Stefan extracted one like a surgeon. The knife glinted under the television lights. In his other hand, he grasped a metal rod that I recognized as a honing steel. With lightning speed, he began to run the knife's blade up and down the steel. It made a high-pitched, scratchy sound, like a sword fight.

"Who can tell me," Stefan said, the blade still swooshing on the steel, "which is more dangerous: a sharp knife or a blunt knife?"

When no one replied, Maura ventured, "A sharp one?"

Wrong answer. It was a trick question. This was the first thing Luís had taught me when I started working the line at Taverna Ristorante.

Stefan stopped sharpening the blade. "Incorrect." Tall Maura seemed to shrink under his flinty gaze. "A dull knife slips off the food and the board. The sharp knife requires less force and is easier to maneuver." Maura's pale cheeks flushed pink. "Now, who knows how to properly hold a knife?"

This time Philip answered. "You grip the end of the blade, not just the handle."

"Very good," replied Stefan. "Would you like to show us how to cut an onion?"

Would he ever. Philip jumped to attention, darting around the table to stand next to Stefan. He took the ten-inch knife, gripping the handle and the heel of the blade between his thumb and forefinger. It was just how Luís held his knife.

Stefan set a whole white onion on the cutting board. Confidently, Philip lopped off the top so the onion wouldn't roll on the cutting board. He peeled the papery skin from the bulb. He sliced it in half, root to top. "Do you want a chop or a dice?" he asked. A cameraman advanced for a close-up of Philip's hands.

"Who knows the difference?" Stefan asked the rest of us.

I was about to answer when Mario did. "Chopped is like chunks. A dice is smaller and more square."

Stefan nodded. "A dice," he instructed Philip.

Philip moved quickly.

"Keep the tip of the knife on the board and use a rocking motion," Stefan directed. He leaned down for a better look at Philip's technique.

Philip slowed down, exaggerating the movements.

"Use your knuckles to guide the blade."

Philip curled the fingers of the hand on the onion into a kind of claw. "This keeps you from cutting off your fingernails," Luís had once told me. I'd been more worried about my fingers than my nails. Nails grow back.

Philip's onion fell into a pile of perfect quarter-inch cubes. The rest of us clapped.

"Why are you not crying?" Stefan asked. "Most people cry when they cut onions, no?" Philip, stumped, looked for a moment like he might start to.

"The sharper the knife, the less you cry," said Shelby. "Or that's what they say."

"Give me a brunoise," said Stefan. He was pacing the length of the two tables where we had spread out to practice our knife skills.

No one had said a word since Stefan had handed us each our own professional-grade starter knife set—a razor-sharp ten-inch chef's knife, a serrated knife, and a short paring knife—and pointed to a basket of produce. Every once in a while, I would raise my eyes from my cutting board to sneak a look at the others. Philip was chopping like a kung-fu master on speed. I had never seen a knife fly like that. Stefan nodded as he watched over Dante's shoulder, then Mario's. Once I looked up and saw Shelby watching me. She quickly looked back down at her zucchini. It seemed everyone was sizing up the competition.

A pile of fairly uniform carrots, zucchini, onions, and celery had accumulated in front of me, but I had no idea what a brunoise was. I didn't even know what language it was, though I guessed French. I could mince, I could dice, I could chop, but could I brun-wha-huh? I wished I'd spent a few more hours with Julia Child before coming.

Hoping someone else might know the answer, my eyes drifted to the others' work stations. Stan was carefully cutting a turnip into what looked like tiny matchsticks, so I started to do the same.

Now Stefan was over my shoulder. "Sophie, that is a julienne. A brunoise is a very fine dice, perfect cubes. It must be consistent."

He started to take my knife out of my hand to demonstrate when a ringing *clang!* filled the room. The sound of knives swooshing against cutting boards instantly stopped, and we all froze. I turned toward the sound, fully expecting someone to be missing a finger or a toe. The knives were sharp enough that I wouldn't be surprised to find someone missing a foot.

It was Maura. Her knife was lying on the floor, just a few inches from her foot. There was no blood, but she was seconds away from bursting into tears, her freckled face pale. To my right, I thought I heard Dante snicker, but I felt bad for Maura as she bent to retrieve the knife, as well as relieved it hadn't been me who'd dropped it. Avoiding eye contact, Maura sheepishly wiped the blade against the white chef's coat embroidered with her name and the *Teen Test Kitchen* logo.

"No!" Stefan shrieked, causing me to jump again. He flew across the kitchen and caught Maura by the wrist just as her knife descended on a head of cabbage. Stefan had a horrible look on his face. "Would you want to eat food that was cut with a knife that had fallen on the floor?" he asked, as appalled as if Maura had just licked the bottom of her shoe. A blush deepened across her cheeks to a shade that, in a crayon box, would be called Mortified Mauve.

"No," she squeaked, the tears brimming.

"The sink is over there," Stefan instructed her, and Maura went to wash the offending utensil.

I gripped my knife for dear life.

The cafeteria was bustling with regular NCA students and instructors. Shelby and I slid into a long buffet line.

"Oooh," she said, reading the menu card beside the first chafing dish. "Truffled mac 'n' cheese and roasted leg of lamb with a sour cherry demi-glace. So I guess we can pretty much expect to leave this place ten pounds heavier?"

"Please," I said, shuffling forward in line. "Like you need to worry about that."

She looked flabbergasted. "I do! I have total cottage cheese thighs."

"I'll trade you cottage cheese thighs for the tank."

"What's the tank?"

"My bu . . . ," I started to explain about my big, fat Greek butt, but faded off as a guy seemed to be walking toward us, smiling. He was *hot*, the sort of hot that made you nervous. He looked younger than many of the other NCA students, maybe only a few years older than us. He was tall, with tousled brown hair and piercingly blue eyes. His skin was a honey-colored tan. There was something about his lips, too. He got in line behind me, and Shelby and I glanced at each other sideways, our eyes popping.

"Hello, Mark," he said to the student spooning mac 'n' cheese. Ooh la la. He had some kind of sexy European accent. "How is it going?"

"Can't complain," said the older guy, who had a goatee and tattoos covering his arms. This seemed to be a popular look at the NCA. "You?"

I risked a look back. Hot tamale, this guy was gorgeous.

For the first time, I understood what romance novels meant by "swooning."

Shelby tugged at my sleeve, and I realized I'd been holding up the line, staring. With my luck, there was a camera catching it all. I blushed and followed Shelby to our *Teen Test Kitchen*–designated seating area in the cafeteria's courtyard. Stan waved us over to a table where he had saved seats. We'd been in Napa one day, and already the eight chefs had broken off into groups. Dante, Mario, and Philip sat together, while Britney and Maura were whispering urgently at their own table. Shelby and I stuck with Stan.

"So what did you think?" he asked as we sat down, meaning our rigorous morning in the kitchen with drill sergeant Stefan.

"Oof," I replied as if I'd been sucker-punched in the stomach.

"I know, seriously, right?" said Stan. "And that was just knife skills."

"Did you guys see Philip?" I asked. We all looked in Philip's direction. He caught us, and we quickly acted like we were talking about something else. "It was like one of those chefs at a hibachi restaurant," I whispered.

"Oh, I love those places!" said Stan. "And you're just saying that because he's Asian."

"No, I'm not!"

"I once found a roach in my hibachi shrimp," said Shelby. She was picking at the spinach, grapefruit, and hazelnut salad with poppy seed dressing next to her lamb, moving all the offending hazelnuts to the side of her tray.

"Philip can pretend he's starring in *Kill Bill 3* all he wants," said Stan, "but Team S is gonna own that kitchen."

"Team S?" asked Shelby.

"Shelby, Stan, and Sophie. But really it's for 'superstar.'" Stan framed his face with jazz hands and arched his eyebrows.

"Can you imagine going here for real?" I asked. In the courtyard, we were a *TTK* island in a sea of extraordinary culinary talent. It was hard not to be intimidated. Only the best of the best went to the NCA.

My gaze settled on a table in the corner—the hot guy from the buffet line. Shelby and Stan caught me staring again and followed my eyes over to him.

Stan approved. "Mmmm, mmmm, good!"

"Seriously," said Shelby. "You know, he looks really familiar. I swear I've seen him before."

"In an underwear ad?" asked Stan hopefully.

"I wish," I said, shoveling a forkload of sinfully rich mac 'n' cheese into my mouth.

Shelby squinted as she thought. "No. . . . I know! He was in that article I read about Napa wineries. That's Jean Renault's son. He owns one of the best vineyards in the valley. They're French, and they've won all sorts of awards."

"French?" purred Stan. "I'd like to sop him up with a piece of baguette."

The water I'd just swallowed almost made a reappearance through my nose. "Stan!"

"What?" he said. "I know you agree with me." That point I had to concede.

Before *Teen Test Kitchen*, I had no idea what a mirepoix was. I had never had use for a mirepoix—or I hadn't known I had use for a mirepoix. A mirepoix sounds complicated. It's not. Here is what a mirepoix is: onion, carrots, and celery. It's a base used to flavor stocks and soups. By the end of our first week on the show, I had chopped and sautéed more carrots, onion, and celery than I cared to think about. I had also boiled, blanched, broiled, poached, roasted, sliced, diced, stirred, and mixed to a point of exhaustion. I had watched Stefan and Chef Bouchard make vegetable soup and fish stew, mash potatoes, fillet a whole fish (not appealing), and debone, stuff, and truss a chicken (even less appealing). I had tried, with varying degrees of success, to replicate these minor culinary miracles on my own.

My vegetable soup was bland, but my fish stew, according to Chef Bouchard, was "complex." I got about three ounces of flesh out of a very unlucky two-pound trout, but I was a natural with the chicken. To be entirely fair, I had a head start. Nonna taught me how to work a chicken when she found out I was going on the show. "Don't be afraid of the chicken," she stressed with a knobby finger bobbing up and down in the air.

The week was a blur revolving around the kitchen. In our morning classes, we were expected to watch and learn every step of whatever technique or recipe was demonstrated. Afternoon labs were spent trying to duplicate those recipes as Stefan barked instructions and eyed our dishes like they were roadkill. At meals in the cafeteria, I'd practically put a crick in my neck tracking the movements of my new crush, Luc Renault. And my exhausted evenings were occupied with the delightful diversions of what Shelby and I had dubbed the Stan Show. More than once that week, I'd collapsed into bed at night with my uniform still on. I had to wonder if sleeplessness was the point. By law, we were only allowed to work on camera a certain number of hours a day, but I couldn't imagine our tightly packed schedule wasn't intentional. Everyone knows sleep deprivation makes for good reality television. By Friday, I barely knew what day it was.

Still, to my surprise, nothing too crazy had happened yet. I kept waiting for someone to crack, to storm out of the kitchen telling Stefan where he could put his ladle (I could think of a few places if they were looking for suggestions). My money was on Maura or Britney. After dropping her knife the first day, Maura cowered in front of Stefan like a mouse in front of a boa constrictor. Stefan seemed to enjoy it. On Tuesday, Britney had burned her potato gratin, and on Wednesday, Chef Bouchard had muttered something in French when he extracted a piece of broken clam shell from her bouillabaisse. It might have been something about her trying to kill him, but I wasn't sure. If only Luc had been around to translate.

The highlight of the week for me—beyond thoroughly trouncing the others at trussing a chicken—had involved him. It was Thursday, and we were taking a short break from filming. The bathroom on our floor was full, so I was hurrying through the main atrium to the one on the first floor. Passing by the reception desk, I smiled at the woman who distributed brochures on Napa and the NCA to tourists. Had she not smiled and waved back, I probably wouldn't have run smack into Luc, coming off the elevator.

"Uh, sorry," I stammered.

"No problem," he said—only with his accent, it came out no *problème.* A smile played at the corners of his mouth. "You are in the television show, right?"

"Yeah, *Test Teen Kitchen.* I mean, *Teen Test Kitchen.*" The familiar blush crept up my neck and cheeks.

He nodded. "I'm Luc. I'm a second-year student."

"Sophie," I said. "I'm on *Teen Test Kitchen* . . . but I just said that. Ha."

I could feel the woman at the visitors' desk watching our exchange with bated breath, our voices, even though low, echoing in the atrium. The elevator behind Luc pinged again, and more students, just released from their morning classes, filed out. They hurried past and around us, and we awkwardly sidestepped them and each other.

We were allowed to turn off our microphones for

bathroom breaks, for the obvious reason that the producers didn't need to hear us pee, but from the second-floor balcony, I saw a cameraman spot me. He raised his camera to his shoulder.

"I better go," I said.

Luc smiled, tipping his chin. "Well, I wish you good luck then. Sophie." He winked and was gone.

On Friday, Stefan clicked a button on a remote control, and a large screen descended from the ceiling at the front of the kitchen. We were gathered to receive our assignment from Tommy, *Charlie's Angels*–style. Tommy wasn't joining us in person, the MIB had told us before we started shooting. He was off being a celebrity chef somewhere—New York, Los Angeles, Las Vegas, Hong Kong, we weren't told—but he would grade Friday's cook-off by live feed. I was curious to see how that would work.

The screen blinked, and Tommy's face appeared. "Good morning, angels," I expected him to say.

"Hello, chefs," he said instead. "You've had a week to take stock of the basics and hone your knife skills. Now the heat is on." The puns were terrible. "Are you ready to show us what you've learned this week?"

"Yes, Chef," we responded on cue.

"Good." Wait for it, wait for it . . . I thought. "Because there will be a test." *Zing!*

Our assignment was to make a dish that showcased the basic techniques we'd learned that week. We had two hours. I tried desperately to think of something original as the giant clock ticked down, but all I kept coming back to was pizza.

It was something I was familiar with but also a blank canvas. The crust was a basic dough: flour, oil, water, salt, and yeast. Then there was a sauce, which included caramelizing onions, sautéing garlic, and simmering tomatoes. Next, toppings, which had to be sliced and diced. Finish it with cheese and bake (another technique), and I figured I had Cooking 101 pie on a pan. Still, it wasn't exciting enough, not for *Teen Test Kitchen*. At home I liked my pizza simple, with nothing but olive oil, fresh tomatoes, basil, and mozzarella. But if I was going to make a dish that could be delivered to every American's home in twenty minutes or less, I had to do something to make it stand out. I had to be daring.

We collectively held our breath as Patricia's knife lowered like a guillotine on Philip's seared scallops in saffron sauce with braised leeks. It was already apparent that Patricia was the bad cop. She had destroyed the three plates before Philip's. Mario's grilled flank steak was "rubbery and dry," Britney's corn and shrimp chowder was "tepid," and even Shelby looked like she might cry when Patricia asked if she had bothered to taste the potatoes under her roast chicken. I had to wonder if Patricia realized we weren't the seasoned chefs she skewered in her magazine every month, but teenagers still getting our footing in the kitchen.

Chef Bouchard had first go at Philip's dish. He nodded appreciatively as he chewed. His job on the panel was to grade our technique, but it was also clear that he was the good cop. For one, he looked like Chef Boyardee and sounded like Pepé Le Pew, which made him inherently likable. In addition, he had taught us firsthand that week, so he knew our abilities and shortcomings as a group and as individuals. There was sympathy there that I didn't see in Patricia.

Chef Bouchard sat back from the table and steepled his hands below his chin. "Philip, your flavors are bright. I think the plate is quite skillful." He turned to Patricia and Stefan, who was seated at the table to taste our dishes and to report on our progress that week, though he wasn't involved in grading. Patricia and Stefan nodded along. "My only complaint," Chef continued, "is that the scallops could have been seared a bit longer. I would have liked more of a crust. Turn up the heat and make sure you pat the scallops dry before you sear them, and I think this dish would be superb. Tommy?"

Virtual Tommy assented. "You taste with your eyes first," Tommy said, "and this dish is inviting. You've got a mix of color and texture. There's the light green of the leeks and the punch of yellow in the saffron sauce. It's just beautiful."

Philip's plate was bright and composed. He'd even drizzled a design with the saffron sauce on the lip of his plate. Tommy had been kind to everyone so far, though. I knew it was killing Stefan, who had not been so generous in our labs.

But all eyes were on Patricia. Her fork and knife poised above the plate, she looked almost brooding as she chewed. She swallowed. "Very flavorful," she pronounced, and I got the feeling she was one of those people who spelled it with a *u*—flavourful.

Philip exhaled. "Thank you, Chef." Mario gave Philip a congratulatory pat on the back that almost sent the slighter boy staggering forward, but he smiled in relief.

Waiters dressed in black whisked in from "offstage," removing Philip's plates and bringing mine. While I could certainly pick apart anything I had cooked, I was happy with my dish. The crust had baked to a nice golden brown, even without a pizza stone, which I was surprised and dismayed to find missing from our kitchen. The dish was certainly not as fancy as Philip's, but I supposed it had a rustic look to it that was inviting.

A waiter set my plates in front of the judges, and my heart sank as one of Patricia's eyebrows went north. "Sophie, you made pizza?" she asked.

"Yes, Chef," I answered. Technically, Patricia was not a chef, at least not in her day job, although she had graduated from the NCA before starting *Foodie*. But the term of address had been so hammered into us that week it had already become a reflex. And I kind of liked it. It made me feel like a pro.

"Flatbreads are underestimated," Patricia said, wielding her cutlery. My hope rose a little, as I tried to determine if this was a compliment or just an observation.

Patricia was a pretty woman, and she knew it. Her dark hair was cut in a stylish bob, and her heavily lined chocolate eyes were wide-set. The toned, skinny arms that acted as a clothes hanger for her designer shirt made it hard to believe she spent a good part of her job eating.

"Tell us about your dish," Tommy said.

"I made a flatbread," I answered, stealing Patricia's word,

as it sounded fancier than pizza, "with a slow-simmered tomato sauce, prosciutto, black olives, and Parmesan."

The panel of judges nodded. Chef Bouchard cut a triangle from his slice of pizza, and I braced myself as he lifted it to his mouth. It was the first time anything I had cooked would be tasted by a professional chef—not counting, of course, Luís—or Stefan, whom I had come to see not as a chef but as a carbuncle on the face of my time in Napa. Never had I depended so much on someone I so disliked.

"Is this your favorite pizza?" Patricia asked.

"I usually make Margherita at home," I replied.

"Why did you decide to do this, then?" Patricia was looking at me with an intensity I was sure the cameras were eating up.

I shrank. "Um . . . I love *prosciutto*." I played up my fancy Italian pronunciation. "And I like olives and Parmesan. I thought they'd work well together." I felt I needed a better story, but it was all I could think of.

"Did they?" she asked.

"Did what?"

"Did you feel the olives and Parmesan worked well with the *prosciutto*?" She mimicked my pronunciation, but whether it was natural or mocking, I couldn't tell.

I stood in front of the panel like a deer caught in headlights.

"What I think Patricia is getting at," said Chef Bouchard, mercifully filling the space created by my silence, "is there was a lot of savory on this pizza. Prosciutto, olives, and Parmesan are all very salty. Your flavors need to be balanced. It would have been nice, for example, to drizzle the salty prosciutto with a balsamic reduction or to use a creamy goat cheese instead of Parmesan. Together, your toppings just didn't work."

"For a pizza, there is just too much going on," Patricia said. "Sometimes the classics are a classic for a reason. There is nothing better than a really good crust—and yours was flawless, Sophie—with just a bright tomato sauce, really good buffalo mozzarella, and fresh basil. Yum."

Tommy chuckled in agreement on the screen. "Don't mess with the classics!" he said. I wanted to ask him if that was his theory when he came up with his signature Spicy Korean Chicken Lollipops.

"Very nice job on the crust, though, Sophie," said Chef Bouchard. "It was the perfect combination of chewy and crunchy. You mastered that lesson."

"I like the rustic feel of the dish," said Tommy. "It makes me want to dig in and tear a piece off."

"Too bad you can't!" said Patricia. I thought I detected a hint of sarcasm. Perhaps Patricia found Tommy's digital setup disappointing too.

Tommy just laughed. "Yes, beam me up, Scottie!"

"Well, thank you, Sophie," Chef Bouchard said.

"Thank you, chefs," I replied, and stepped down from the firing line.

"That was rough," Shelby said. "How could I forget salt?"

It was later that night, and Team S was slumped in our normal spot on the patio behind the dorm. Philip, who seemed to have distanced himself slightly from Mario and Dante over the course of the week, to my surprise, had joined us. He sat next to Stan, and the contrast was amusing. Where Stan was large, in size and in mannerisms, Philip was small and contained, though equally well dressed. He was cute, if maybe a little neurotic. As the winner of the first cook-off, with his saffron scallops, I would have thought he'd be euphoric, but Philip was berating himself for the judges' criticisms just as much as the rest of us.

He said, "I thought to myself, Philip, maybe you should let the scallops sear a little more. There's no room for impatience in the kitchen." His distress was real.

"Phil," Stan said, laying a paw on Philip's slight shoulder, "go easy on yourself. You won."

"Yeah, and you won an iPad," I offered. Philip's prize was loaded with all the food- and recipe-related apps you could think of.

"I already have an iPad." Philip pouted. "And besides, I can't get my hands on it until after the show. What good does that do me now?"

"Philip, don't make us hate you," said Shelby.

You knew it was a rough day when you had to console the winner.

Chapter Six

By Saturday, I was ready for a hall pass away from the NCA campus for a couple of days. Technically, weekends were our "down days," but that didn't mean the producers were going to miss any potential drama. On Saturdays and Sundays, a smaller "second unit" of two cameramen would stick around just in case a catfight or a ratings-making meltdown erupted.

The producers had arranged a van into nearby St. Helena for anyone who wanted to go, but I'd decided I needed a break from my fellow cheftestants and our entourage. I'd finally been able to call my dad that morning. Feeling miserable, I rehashed my failed "flatbread." Hearing his voice so far away, I felt the distance of my family more than I had since I'd arrived in California. I wondered how he was doing without me at the restaurant and how Nonna and Pappou were. He had no news from Alex. Perhaps hearing the homesickness in my voice, he reminded me that my aunt was just down the road. It may have been seven years since I'd seen Aunt Mary, but I was hoping even a vaguely familiar face might cheer me up.

Leaving campus without the group, however, required clearance from the producers. They needed to know where I was going, with whom, and for how long. It wasn't going to be easy to escape the show's clutches, but when I told the MIB about Aunt Mary and her restaurant, his eyes lit up at the potential of a side story. "Let me check with the story producer," he said, whoever that spectral figure was.

In the end, they okayed it. Of course, under my nondisclosure agreement, I wasn't allowed to talk about the show with anyone, including my aunt. I would have to be back by five P.M., and I was not allowed to take or bring back any materials. And Aunt Mary would have to sign a release because they were sending a camera with me. I wondered if this was what it felt like to be on parole.

Aunt Mary's restaurant was not far from the NCA. It had a starred review in a restaurant guide to Napa I picked up from the school's visitors' desk:

> ★ **The Last Supper.** New American.
> **Award-winning chef Mary Harris believes every meal should be enjoyed as if it were your last. Harris clearly respects her ingredients. Her deft yet unaffected celebration of the valley's best produce and locally sourced surf and turf might just have you thinking you've gone to heaven.**

When I called her at the number I'd scribbled on my hand, the MIB was listening in. To make sure I wasn't smuggling culinary secrets or leaking spoilers, I suspected, but it made my first conversation with my aunt in years a little awkward.

"Sophia!" she exclaimed at the sound of my voice. "Your father e-mailed me to say you would be out here. For that show! He didn't say much else, though."

"Yeah," I said, glancing at the MIB. "We're not really allowed to talk about it. But we have the weekends off, and I was thinking maybe—"

"You should come out to the restaurant!" she said before I could float the idea myself. "Tomorrow?"

"Sure. Yeah. I'd like to see it." I gnawed at a hangnail on the side of my thumb.

"Great! Oh, Sophia, I'll be so glad to see you. Should I pick you up, say around ten?"

"The restaurant is just down the road from the NCA, right?"

"Less than a mile."

"I can walk. If that's okay." I looked at the MIB, who hesitated, considering the logistics, and then nodded.

"Are you sure?" asked Aunt Mary.

"Yeah. I could use some fresh air. It's gorgeous out here, and all I see is the inside of a kitchen!"

Aunt Mary chuckled. "I like to walk myself, when I can."

"Oh, and Aunt Mary"—I hesitated before hanging up—"it's Sophie now. Only my dad and grandparents call me Sophia."

Aunt Mary laughed again, and it was an oddly familiar sound, a laugh I knew, a laugh I'd heard before, years ago. Already I felt better.

The shoulder on the side of the road really wasn't wide enough for two people. That didn't stop the cameraman from walking beside me, his lens pointed directly at my face. My reasons for wanting to walk to my aunt's restaurant did not entirely have to do with exercise and sunshine. I had hoped walking might deter a cameraman carrying fifty pounds of equipment from following me. No such luck. He lumbered along beside me sweating profusely and dropping a few steps behind whenever a van or rental car whizzed past. Occasionally he ran out in front of me or panned the horizon.

I tried to enjoy the scenery and the blissfully sunny day and ignore the camera ruining my view of Napa's gently sloping hills. The farther I got from the NCA, the better I felt—the opposite of my experience just a week before, as I had arrived for the show. I'd had no idea what kind of pressure I'd feel not just studying at one of the world's best culinary institutes and competing against some of the country's best teen chefs, but doing it under the constant scrutiny of a television camera. Walking down the road, past fields of gnarled grapevines planted in neat rows under a bright blue Napa sky, it was like a weight lifted off my shoulders.

The peace was interrupted when a car slowed beside me. I expected it was in response to an SOS from the cameraman, who'd fallen a good ten yards behind me. Instead,

I turned to find Luc hanging out of the passenger-side window of a Mini Cooper. He grinned, squinting slightly from the sun in his eyes.

"Hello, Sophie. Going somewhere?" he asked.

There was a man in the car with him with the same blue eyes and dark, tousled hair, only his had streaks of gray. He watched me with vague curiosity as the car idled.

"I'm going to visit my aunt. She has a restaurant down the road."

"I see. So they let the elephants out of the circus for the weekend?"

I hoped it was just lost in translation. Nervously I glanced back at the cameraman, who was on his cell phone now.

Luc saw him too. "Can we give you a ride?"

I peered down the highway; the road where I was supposed to turn for the restaurant wasn't even in sight yet. "It's not so far," I lied.

"Okay," Luc relented, withdrawing back into the car.

"Hey, kid!" the cameraman yelled.

"On second thought . . ." I got into the car.

"Hey, kid!"

"Would your friend like a lift?" the older man asked, glancing in the rearview mirror with an amused smile.

I looked back. The cameraman was jogging toward us. The front of his T-shirt was soaked in a dark V. "Yeah," I sighed. "I guess we should. If you don't mind."

With the ripe cameraman and his bulky equipment wedged into the back seat beside me, I was glad the ride to the restaurant was short. Luc made introductions. The man who bore a striking resemblance was, as I had suspected, his father, Jean Renault.

"Our vineyard is just up the road," Mr. Renault said as we pulled into the small parking lot beside the Last Supper.

"You should see it sometime," Luc said.

"Okay." I blushed, wondering if he was just being polite.

"Enjoy your day, Sophie." I liked how Luc always said my name—"Hello, Sophie." "How are you, Sophie?" "Enjoy your day, Sophie."

"You too," I said. "Thank you, Mr. Renault, for the ride."

"Thanks," the cameraman added as he awkwardly poured out of the car and straightened himself.

Luc and Mr. Renault waved as they drove away, and suddenly I was nervous, not about Luc but about something else. I was actually going to see my aunt, my mom's sister. What were we going to talk about after all these years? I couldn't discuss the show. And she and my dad didn't keep up much. Would she even recognize me?

"Sophia?"

I turned at the sound of my aunt's voice. She was standing in the entrance of the restaurant with a kitchen towel slung over her shoulder. She looked so much like the photos of my mother.

"Sorry. Sophie," she corrected herself, the skin at the corners of her blue eyes crinkling with a smile as she came toward me.

I remembered her with long hair hanging down past her shoulders, but it was short now and wavy. She wore a lavender shirt over flowy black pants and Crocs. And before I could say anything, she was hugging me. "It's so good to see you."

"You too," I mumbled into her shoulder.

She drew back and looked at my face as if she was memorizing it, or remembering it.

"I've got company." I nodded apologetically toward the cameraman, who was cursing and changing the battery on his camera.

"I figured you might," she said. "Come in."

I followed her through the trellised entry into the restaurant. It was cozy inside. Heavy rustic wood beams ran across the ceiling. At one end, a giant wood-burning stove yawned under a gleaming copper hood. It was the kind of romantic place where I imagined girls found engagement rings in their desserts. Worlds away from Taverna Ristorante's family dining.

"It's getting hot out there," said Aunt Mary, fanning herself with her hand. "You walked?"

"I got a lift from . . . a friend," I said.

"Jean Renault? I saw him pull out of the parking lot. How do you know him?"

"I don't really. I know his son. Or I've met his son."

"Luc's on the show?"

"No, he's a student at the NCA," I said, wanting to change the subject. The cameraman had followed us in, his camera locked and loaded and ready to shoot.

Aunt Mary disappeared behind a partition that separated the dining room from the kitchen, and I followed. The kitchen was relatively small but spotless. While modern, it had a homey, rustic air similar to the restaurant's dining room. Copper pots on hooks lined one wall.

Standing at a table, a man in jeans with a goatee and a ponytail was writing on a whiteboard.

"Sophie, this is Rick. Rick, this is my niece Sophie. Rick's my right-hand man." Rick smiled at me. "He's planning the night's menu. Did Greenbrier's bring that crate of cherries?"

Rick stroked his chin. "Not yet. If not, I'm thinking maybe we could use those blackberries we got from Andy."

Aunt Mary considered this substitution. "Not exactly what I was thinking, but if they're nice. . . . I'll see what I can find at the market." She turned to me. "I was hoping we could just catch up, but I have to go to the farmers' market for tonight. Our buyer called in with a sprained ankle. Would you mind coming with me? I figured it might be fun for you."

I brightened. I loved the farmers' market in DC that I always dragged Alex to, and I'd read that the ones in Napa were fantastic.

"Grab a basket," Aunt Mary said, pointing to a stack of them in the corner. I threaded two on my arms and skipped off like Little Red Riding Hood going to Grandma's house.

There's nothing in this world better than ripe, sun-warmed summer tomatoes. The tomato-like red balls of mush you buy at the grocery store are a bad imitation, the karaoke version of your favorite song. I was drawing this comparison as Aunt Mary wound her way through the crowded farmers' market to a low stone wall, where she laid out a small spread of some of the treasures we had found: half a loaf of freshly baked French bread, a slab of sheep's milk cheese, local olives, and two deep red peaches. The yeasty aroma of the bread made my mouth water. In fact, the whole market did. It reminded me of the stories my grandmother told about market day when she was a girl in Italy.

Every stall overflowed with color and tantalizing smells. There were vegetable vendors and flower vendors and local dairies with hand-pulled mozzarella and milk in glass bottles. There were brown eggs, white eggs, pinky-orange eggs, greeny-blue eggs, spotted eggs. PICKED TODAY, read one handwritten sign taped to a crate of fragrant strawberries. There was a man selling organic beef and a fisherman with a cooler full of Pacific halibut and one woman who sold twelve different kinds of honey. And there were samples everywhere, even a small band playing. It was one big, bustling celebration of food.

Aunt Mary tore a hunk of bread from the loaf and topped it with a healthy slice of cheese. I sat beside her on the wall, wiping the sweet tangy juices of a peach from my chin. She took a sip of wine, a Cabernet Sauvignon, she told me, from none other than Luc's family vineyard, Clos d'Été.

"How's your father?" She squinted against the afternoon sun, even under the brim of her floppy straw hat.

"He's okay," I replied. "The restaurant keeps him busy."

My aunt nodded as if she understood that statement more than anyone. "And your grandparents?"

"They're getting old. But they're fine. Nonna's still keeping Pappou in line."

My aunt smiled. "And what about you?"

"I'm good."

"Any special boys in your life?"

The cameraman had momentarily detached himself from us to capture some of the scene. I could see him cutting an awkward swath through the crowd. Still, I hesitated. Luc was just a crush, and if my aunt knew his father, I couldn't be sure she wouldn't say something to him. But I did think of Alex. "There's one." Aunt Mary perked up. "But he's just a friend. Well, my best friend."

"You must miss him."

"I do." With the grueling pace of the last week, I'd barely had time to think about Alex. But with a sharp pang where my heart was, I realized how much I did miss him. There were so many things I wanted to tell him about, like Philip's funny way of humming pop songs to himself as he cooked, or how Mario seemed to view the show as one big infomercial for his family's new line of salsas—he always found ways to mention their "all-natural ingredients" or their "new peach-jalapeño flavor!" Or how Maura sounded like Luna Lovegood from the Harry Potter movies and how Dante also loved the Poes, Alex's favorite band. I had to keep these things on a mental checklist I could tell him when this was all over.

"Sometimes it's good to miss someone," said Mary. I wondered if she was talking about my mother.

We sat in silence for a few minutes and watched the people shopping and sampling, some just milling around. I wished I could stay there all day, lost in the mix without Stefan or a camera looking over my shoulder. For the first time since I'd gotten to Napa, I felt normal.

“Well,” my aunt said finally, slapping her hands on her knees. “Shall we go?” The cameraman was picking his way back toward us. “I need to get our take back to Rick. I can show you the gardens too. We just planted a new herb tub this spring.”

“You have gardens at the restaurant?”

“Yep. Out back. A lettuce patch, herbs, some vegetables and fruit trees. Nothing too fancy. Plus a few chickens to keep things lively.”

“You have chickens?”

“Uh-huh. We mostly trade the eggs.”

“Wow,” I said. “You’ve got everything you need right there.”

“Well, not everything certainly, but we farm what we can. The shorter the distance from the ground to the table, the better.”

“Hmmm. I guess I’d always thought the shorter the distance from the plate to my mouth, the better.”

Aunt Mary laughed and put her arm around me. For a second, I felt like I was home.

Week 2

FRENCH CUISINE

Chapter Seven

You really can't talk about French food without talking about wine. It's as fundamental to French cooking as olive oil is to Mediterranean fare or butter is to Southern food. And since our second week in the Test Kitchen was all about French cuisine, we were going on a field trip to Clos d'Été—Luc's family winery. In the car Luc had mentioned he worked at the vineyard three days a week. As our van pulled up the cypress-lined driveway to a French-style château nestled between rolling vineyards, I prayed Monday was one of those days.

"Is that a castle?" Dante asked.

"I feel like I'm in a fairy tale," Britney gushed.

"Totally," said Mario.

If this was a fairy tale, I knew who was Prince Charming.

Behind the château, which housed the winery's tasting

room, lab, business office, and the Renault family's private home, there was an even larger building where the grapes were pressed, fermented, aged in huge oak barrels, and finally, bottled. The cameras rolled as we followed Jean Renault through the tour and peered over the railings into the workings of the winery below. My favorite, however, was the underground wine cave, where the barrels were stored for aging. The sloping stone walls and the musty smell of oak reminded me of the Greek Orthodox church my father took Raffi and me to on Christmas and Easter.

"Why do you store them underground?" Philip asked.

"Good question," answered Jean. Philip had been full of them. "Caves allow us to control the temperature and the humidity of the air while the wines are aging. This affects the taste of the wine. Using underground space also leaves more land aboveground for planting."

"Have you told them about the angels' share?" a voice behind us said.

"No. Do you want to?"

Luc must have snuck in behind us. I turned to find him leaning on an upright barrel in the dim light of the cave. "The angels' share is what they call the alcohol that evaporates through the barrels into the air," he explained. "Even an angel needs to be bad once in a while." He winked at me as he said it.

"Trust me. It will *feel* authentic," the MIB was assuring one of the winery workers. They were helping set up four large vats of grapes that we would soon be trampling like a herd of water buffalo.

Luc looked unconvinced. He sighed and whispered in my ear, "The harvest—the 'crush,' we call it—isn't until fall. We use machines now anyway. Do you know how many people it would take to stomp a year's worth of wine?"

I shrugged. "The magic of television!"

Somehow I had been selected as the guinea pig for a grape-stomping lesson from Luc. We both stood barefoot with our jeans rolled up around our knees, waiting for the crew to finish assembling the backdrop. I couldn't help but think of the famous scene from *I Love Lucy*, or that YouTube video where the woman falls out of the stomping vat and topples to the ground, bleating like a cow in labor. Dear Bacchus, god of wine, I prayed, please just let me stay upright.

"Okay," the MIB shouted, clapping for everyone's attention. "Sophie, Luc is going to show you how to stomp the grapes, and then everyone else will join in."

"Action!" someone yelled. Luc stepped into the vat. I followed. The grapes squished under my weight, oozing between my toes. I was reminded of a Halloween haunted house I'd been to as a kid, where we'd been blindfolded and our hands plunged into a bowl of "eyeballs and guts"—peeled grapes and cold spaghetti.

"How does it feel?" Luc asked, stomping away. For all his hesitation at the authenticity of this exercise, he sure seemed to be enjoying it now.

"Sort of gross."

"Twist your foot this way." He stomped and swiveled, like a Greek folk dance. I did the same. The grapes made a wet sucking sound, causing Britney (and therefore Mario) to giggle on the sidelines.

"Pretend it's a fire," Luc said, "and you're trying to put it out with your feet."

I stomped wildly until, suddenly, I slipped. I would have gone the way of the YouTube woman had Luc not grabbed me by the arm. "Careful," he said, steadying me.

I held his elbows as we both continued stomping, mashing the fruit under our feet. At one point, our toes brushed each other. It was just for a second. We were still holding on to each other's arms, ostensibly for balance, but it was our feet touching that sent an electric jolt through my body.

"Now you've got it," Luc said. "Only twenty more pounds of grapes, and you've got a gallon of wine!"

I wanted to say something witty in return, but all that came to me was "*I Love Luc-y*," and that seemed both cheesy and creepy. I was also aware of the cameraman circling like a vulture. How, I wondered, was a girl supposed to flirt, with a camera in her face?

"Okay!" the MIB called, and the camera backed off. "Everyone in!"

The moment was over. Luc stepped out of the vat. I expected his feet to be stained purple, but they were only wet and covered with grape skins and seeds.

Shelby took his place in the vat with me. "That," she said, wiggling her eyebrows, "looked romantic."

By my third Kitchen Confidential, I thought I'd gotten the hang of our video diaries. The MIB had passed interviewing responsibilities to Megan, the assistant producer who'd showed us around the first day. She sat across from me with a clipboard on her lap. I tried to read what was written on it, but it was tilted toward her.

"Tell me a little about your trip to the winery today," she said.

"The winery was awesome. It's gorgeous. They showed us all the rooms where the wine is made and stored. They have real caves where they keep the barrels while the wine ages."

"What was your favorite part?"

"The grape stomping was really fun."

I thought I saw a smile twitch at the corners of her mouth. "You did that with Luc, the winery owner's son?"

"Yeah." I blushed, unfortunately. Had I walked into a trap?

"What do you think of him?"

"I mean—yeah—Luc's cute—but no—I mean . . ." I clamped my lips together.

Megan cocked an eyebrow. "Is there a guy at home?"

"No. Well, there's Alex."

"Who's Alex?"

Hearing his name out loud, something I was used to hearing every day, made me miss him more. "Alex is my best friend, but . . ."

How far was I willing to go with this diary thing? Did I really want to tell the world about my crush on my best friend? Did I really want to tell Alex? Not on national television, thanks.

"But . . . ?" Megan prodded.

"He's a friend, but that's all." It seemed a safe enough answer.

She jotted something down on her clipboard. "What's your experience with French cooking?" she asked.

I was grateful for the change of topic, even if my answer was "none."

The main thing I had gathered three days into our second week was that the French know how to eat. Chef Bouchard was walking us through a cheese tasting.

"You know, I would trade my firstborn child for a wheel of real triple-cream Brie," Stan said. His eyes practically rolled back in his head as he deposited a healthy wedge of the rich cheese on his tongue. "Particularly if it came with a jar of French fig preserves."

I knew what he meant. The day before we'd had a chocolate tasting, and the raspberry truffle I tried was the closest thing to a religious experience I'd ever had.

All eight of us crowded around the cheese tray. You would have thought we were a group of prisoners off a hunger strike.

"I still prefer *queso*," said Mario, sniffing suspiciously at a sliver of pungent Camembert. "Salsa Mamacita makes a *queso blanco*," he told Britney, who smiled vaguely. It had become clear to everyone, including Britney, that Mario liked her. She did not appear to return his feelings, but she was more than happy to put his crush to good use. She'd bat her eyelashes, and he'd walk her through a technique she hadn't grasped that morning; she'd laugh at one of his jokes, and he'd peel her carrots when she was running short on time. Everyone else just rolled their eyes, but Shelby found it difficult to watch. "She has him wrapped around her little finger," she'd grumble. "I hate to see a good man whipped." Really, I thought, Shelby just hated to see anyone get extra help.

Now Shelby took the opportunity to toy with Britney. "You know you can eat the rind, right, Britney?" she asked pointedly.

Britney had been making a small pile of the cheeses' papery white rinds on the table in front of her. Slitting her eyes at Shelby, she replied, "Of course. I was just saving them." To prove it, she popped a piece of rind in her mouth.

"It's actually a mold," Shelby said, watching with delight as Britney's defiant smile fell into a kind of grimace.

"It's the same genus as the mold used to make penicillin," said Philip.

"*Penicillium*," Shelby added.

"That is correct." Philip sounded like the host of a quiz show. "Discovered by Louis Pasteur."

"No," said Shelby. "By Alexander Fleming. But he didn't discover the mold; he just discovered penicillin."

"That's what I meant," said Philip.

"I'm sure," Shelby replied, the sarcasm dripping like honey.

Philip pursed his lips and turned back to the cheese. "I'm in AP Biology," he said, plucking a dried fig from the plate. "My parents want me to be a doctor."

"Ugh." Stan groaned. "My dad's a doctor. He's done half of Park Avenue's breasts. Most boring job ever. Run while you still can."

"I intend to," Philip replied. "When I win the show, my parents will see my future's in culinary, not medical school."

"*When* you win the show?" repeated Shelby.

Dante and I exchanged a glance over the table. Dante didn't say much, but I thought he, like me, just wanted to fly under the radar. We knew the producers would have a field day with flare-ups like these. Shelby, on the other hand, loved the drama of competition. It only motivated her more.

"I suppose I should say *if*," Philip allowed, "but . . ." He let the word hang in the air.

"We'll see," Shelby said. She tossed her long brown hair over her shoulder and threw the rest of the piece of cheese she'd been nibbling into the trash can. I knew we'd be hearing about this later.

"Cancan is a little dance dance, come and do this cancan right along with me, la da da da da da da." Stan's raw whole chicken did the cancan down the stainless-steel work table in the middle of the kitchen, kicking out its stumpy legs. Stan had even ruffled a paper towel around its "waist" as a makeshift skirt.

Stan and I were delirious with stress and lack of sleep. Shelby and Philip's building rivalry had sucked the air out of the room one too many times that week. After the cheese tasting, there'd been a moment I thought they might actually throw down over green beans amandine. We had to find some way to relieve the pressure. And if having our roasters perform a dramatic interpretation of *Moulin Rouge* took the edge off, so be it. Stan's bird reached the end of the stainless-steel table, twirled, and shimmied its white meat breasts.

"Do the funky chicken!" Mario called. It seemed we all could use a little comic relief—all of us except Shelby and Philip, who were too engrossed in trussing their birds to be amused by us idiots.

"That's just fowl, Stan," I joked.

"Oh, honey, I'm gonna pretend you didn't say that."

"Stan, you're gonna give us all salmonella," Shelby protested. She tugged at her butcher's twine.

Stan stuck out his tongue. "*Coq au wah.*"

Maura giggled just as Stefan walked back into the kitchen. The MIB had called him outside to speak as we started our lab. Stefan looked irritated. He eyed the bird in Stan's hands. "Stan, what are you doing?"

"Nothing, Chef," said Stan, instantly serious. He patted the napkin skirt against the poultry's pimply pink skin. "Just cleaning my chicken."

"It's like babysitting," Stefan spat under his breath. "You should be trussing now."

"Yes, Chef," Stan answered obediently.

It was clear that Stefan's patience was wearing thin. He'd been acting even shorter with us than usual, and more than once that week, signs of an ugly temper had peeked through.

"The pantry is out of white onions," Stefan announced to no one in particular. "Sophie," he barked, "I need you to go down to the cellar and send up a basket."

The cellar was where the school stored fruits and vegetables harvested from its gardens and delivered daily by local farmers. Each kitchen at the NCA was connected to the basement by a dumbwaiter, but I hadn't been down there since our tour of the school the first day. The ingredients we needed for each day's lesson were usually sent up before class, by whom I wasn't sure—I pictured tiny kitchen elves.

"Just one basket. You can take the elevator," Stefan said.

The basement was eerily quiet and, with no natural light and beige tiling, resembled a hospital corridor. There was a storeroom for dry goods, a huge walk-in freezer and refrigerator (there were smaller ones attached to each kitchen), and a root cellar for produce. When I opened the door to the root cellar, I was hit with a deeply earthy smell. It was cool and damp. As my eyes adjusted to the dim light, I saw the shelves were lined with cardboard boxes of vegetables, each labeled with a delivery date. I was surprised to find that part of the long room actually had a dirt floor.

The door behind me creaked and I jumped, my already overtaxed mind filling with images of root cellar homicide. But it was Luc, and he looked equally surprised to see me.

"Sophie!"

"Hi."

We both laughed uncomfortably.

"Stefan sent me down to get onions," I explained.

"Ah, yes. The lift is broken, and I believe the *sous-sol* crew may have—how do you say it? Uh . . . slacked . . . a little on their jobs."

"*Sous-sol*?"

"Sorry. French for . . ." He held his hands out to gesture around the room. "Like a cave?"

"Cellar. Or basement."

He snapped his fingers, grinning. "Yes. Sorry, sometimes my English escapes me."

"It seems pretty good to me." We both smiled and nodded until the silence became awkward. "That wine cave was really cool the other day," I offered.

His grin grew. "It's my favorite place in the winery. It's quiet; one can think there."

"Did you grow up at Clos d'Été? That place is amazing!"

"No, I grew up with my mother in Paris. I came to Napa last year to learn the wine business and study here."

"You were living in Paris! Didn't you want to go to Le Cordon Bleu?" I thought wistfully of the famous Parisian cooking school where Julia Child trained.

"I've been eating French food all my life. It's so . . . stuffy? Cream and butter and eggs. I want to taste the food. I want to be playful."

I listened, charmed by the passion he so evidently felt when it came to cooking. A light had come on in his eyes.

"Do you know Alice Waters?" he asked.

I nodded. "Well, I mean I don't know her, but I know she has a restaurant near San Francisco."

"Chez Panisse, yes. She took the best of French cooking and made it fresh again." His hands flew up in an excited gesture that was flamboyantly European. It was the same way my father and grandparents sometimes spoke with their hands. "I want to do the same," he continued intently. "Not just with French techniques, but with techniques from all over the world. And take it back to France. I want to open a restaurant one day."

"So you'll go back? To France?"

"It's my home." He shrugged.

"Right." In the moment of very loud silence that followed,

I managed to step backward into a crate of red potatoes. "Whoops." I laughed nervously at my own clumsiness as I stooped to pick up the potatoes that had toppled to the floor.

"The show is going well?" Luc pointed to my mic pack. "Or you cannot talk about it?" He raised a dramatic eyebrow.

Our microphones didn't work in the walk-in refrigerators. The thick metal walls blocked the signal—we knew because the MIB had scolded Maura and Britney for having a conversation in there. So I suspected my mic didn't work in the root cellar either. Still, I wondered if there might be a camera. While that sounded paranoid, frankly, I was. "Yeah," I replied with exaggerated enthusiasm, just in case. "I'm learning a lot."

"I am sure you are. Although, how do you handle the cameras all the time! They call it reality, but . . ." He shrugged, his eyes widening as he laughed at the ridiculousness of it.

"You get used to them, I guess." Though clearly I hadn't.

"You would like to be famous?" Luc asked.

"No! I mean not for being on TV." I didn't want him to think I was some kind of fame monger, plotting her post-show publicity circuit and sponsorship deals as she tried to stretch her fifteen minutes. "I mean, that's not why I'm doing it. I don't really like all the attention, but this is my chance. I want to be a chef."

"Ahhh, and here I thought you were a chef already." He winked and looked at me in a way only Alex had looked at me before, as if he saw something in me that I didn't yet. "So, you needed something?" he asked.

I had almost forgotten what Stefan had sent me down to the basement for. "Onions," I blurted. "White ones."

Luc reached toward a shelf, pulling down a bushel and then the one behind it.

"Oh, I only need one," I said.

He placed the first bushel back on the shelf and handed me the second one. "First in, first out," he said. "The newer produce goes to the back. We are supposed to use the older first, but I trust you won't tell anyone. This competition is cutneck, right?" He winked.

I laughed, holding the heavy basket awkwardly in front of me. "Cutneck. Yes." I figured I'd let that one slide.

"Well, good luck with your onions, Sophie."

It was weird that the first person I wanted to tell about my encounter with Luc was Alex. It wasn't weird that I wanted to talk to him, of course, but that I wanted to talk to him about a boy. I didn't talk about guys with Alex. It just never came up. The one time I'd gone out with someone—Greg Shipman the year before, for a whopping two months—Alex and I had spoken Greg's name twice: when he asked me out and when we broke up. There was Greg on one hand and Alex on the other, but the two of them in the same mental space was uncomfortable, like a too-crowded room.

I had never asked Alex for boy advice before, so I didn't understand why I wanted his opinion so much now. Not just about Luc, but about all of it. I wanted to tell him about Shelby and Stan, who were the only ones keeping me sane, although Shelby's competitiveness was starting to wear on me. I wanted to tell him about Stefan's increasing hostility and how I'd only seen Tommy Chang in person once. I wanted to tell him about my aunt and how nervous I was for the second test tomorrow. But our phone calls were limited to family.

If I couldn't get Alex's opinion on Luc, however, I would get Team S's.

"There she is, Miss Greek-Italian America!" Stan sang as I walked toward what had become our lunch table.

I set my tray down and waved my hand at the wrist like an old-school beauty queen. "I'm totally exhausted," I said, plopping into a chair.

"Tell me about it." Shelby sighed. Her elbow was propped on the table, and her head was in her palm. Her lunch looked untouched.

"But something happened today," I volunteered, unable to hide my smile.

Stan straightened up. "Stefan appeared to you in the walk-in as the devil incarnate. Forked tongue, host of demons, black smoke. I knew it." He threw his fork down and sat back in his seat, as if all of his suspicions had been confirmed.

I laughed. "No, but I did see someone when Stefan sent me to the cellar. . . ."

"Who?" Shelby and Stan asked at once, both fully alert now, their eager eyes boring into me.

Maura and Britney were sitting at the table next to ours. They were talking about the ratatouille on the lunch menu that day. "I feel like eggplant is a really happy vegetable," Maura was saying. They weren't listening.

"Luc," I said.

Stan gasped. "Did you kiss him?"

"What? No, Stan! I barely know him."

"Well, you kind of know him," said Shelby. "He did pick

you up on the road the other day—no white stallion, but it's a start. And you guys totally had chemistry at the winery. It was palpable, Sophie."

"Totally palpable," Stan agreed. "I thought you might make out right there."

"Really?" I crinkled my nose, so obviously euphoric over the prospect of chemistry with Luc that it was embarrassing. "You think so? Did I tell you they asked me about him in my Kitchen Confidential?"

"No!" Stan gasped again. "What did you say?"

I squirmed. "I don't know. That he was cute, but . . ."

"But what?" asked Shelby.

Now I was confused. "I don't know. I don't know," I repeated, shaking my head. "They asked me about Alex too." I'd told Shelby and Stan about my complicated relationship with Alex.

"The plot thickens," said Stan. "What'd you say about Alex?"

"Nothing! That he's my best friend, that's all."

"Sounds like he's more than that," Stan said suspiciously.

Shelby cocked her head and eyed me appraisingly. "Alex. Or Luc," she said.

"Huh?"

"I'm trying to figure out which one is more your type, Alex or Luc."

Stan tilted his head also, and they examined me like an exotic ingredient they weren't quite sure what to do with.

"Guys!" I said, feeling uncomfortable. "Come on. I don't know."

"Well, if you had to choose one, which would it be?" asked Shelby.

I sighed and let myself, for a second, imagine both unlikelihoods. "They're so different. I mean, it's like burgers versus coq au vin, the Donut Den versus . . . Le Bernardin. They're both great, just . . . different tastes."

"I'll say," Stan said, always willing to milk any double entendre.

Shelby rolled her eyes. "You're incorrigible, Stan."

He sent an air kiss in her direction. "But you love me for it."

What surprised me most about French cuisine was that it actually wasn't that hard. The dishes we watched Chef Bouchard make that week all seemed to start from the same building blocks. You stuffed one meat into another meat and then slathered it with a sauce. I was no stranger to sauces—tomato, alfredo, pesto, puttanesca—but the French seemed to have an entire family tree of sauces. They all started with egg yolks, stock, or butter and then were seasoned, emulsified, thickened, and thinned into character.

My father once told me the true test of a chef was his egg, so by the time Tommy delivered his "there will be a test" tagline on Friday, I knew what I was going to make. Eggs Benedict was Alex's go-to at Pauline's, our favorite brunch place around the corner from his house. It was not, strictly speaking, a French dish, but we'd made the devilishly rich hollandaise sauce in Chef Bouchard's class on Tuesday. Furthermore, it was a classic, and after my flatbread fiasco,

I wanted to show the judges that I could leave well enough alone.

Stefan was making laps around the kitchen, inspecting each chef's progress as the glowing red clock ticked down to zero. "Your choice of dish is brave," he informed me with a sniff as he peered into my saucepan.

Hollandaise is a tricky emulsion and can take years to perfect. It's made by whisking egg yolks and lemon juice over very low heat until they're smooth and thick, then whisking in melted butter. If the temperature is too high, the yolks can scramble; if you add the butter too quickly, the sauce can separate into a slimy, lumpy mess.

The feeling in the kitchen was tense. No one wanted a repeat of Patricia's slaughter.

"Where did those peaches go?" Dante asked, emerging from the pantry.

"I'm using them for my crepes," said Britney. She was standing over a saucepan, reducing a mixture of orange juice, peaches, and honey.

"You used them all?"

Britney looked up from the stove. "I need them all."

"Britney, you're not the only one cooking here. I needed some of those peaches for my compote." I hadn't heard Dante speak this much or this harshly in the kitchen before. He normally kept to himself, head bowed, diligent except for the occasional aside to Mario.

"I didn't know you needed them," Britney protested.

"I didn't know you were using them all," Dante shot back. Slinging a kitchen towel over his shoulder, he pushed brusquely past Mario. Britney stuck her tongue out at his back.

"Dude," Mario called after Dante, "she didn't know you needed them."

I didn't have time for their drama. My yolks were thickening. Slowly I drizzled in a cup of clarified butter and whisked until the sauce looked like yellow cake batter. I added the tiniest pinch of salt and cayenne pepper and tasted. Too much lemon. Hoping to balance out the acid, I added more butter. To my horror, the sauce began to break.

"No, no, no!" I pleaded under my breath, whisking frantically. "Stan," I hissed. He was working at the station in front of mine on his tart Niçoise.

"Stan," I whispered again. Nervously I glanced in the direction of the closest cameraman, but he hadn't heard me or didn't care about my slimy sauce, because he was filming Maura clumsily trying to pry open an oyster.

"Stan," I hissed one more time. He finally turned, sweaty and red-faced from pitting olives. "My hollandaise broke. How do I fix it?"

Stan's mouth puckered into a concerned O.

"Not helping!" I said.

He pondered for a second. "Whisk like crazy."

"I am!" I said, nodding down at my arm, which was rotating so fast I felt like it was about to come out of the socket.

"Try adding a teeny tiny bit of water."

Stefan was coming our way. I rushed to the sink and let cold water trickle into the bowl. Then I whisked like my life depended on it. My forearms burned. "Come on, come on, come on," I chanted, my eyes closed. I opened them again and looked down. I owed Stan.

And apparently, I wasn't the only one. While Dante and Britney had been sparring over peaches, I'd overheard Stan offer Philip some of the olives he'd claimed for his tart. It wasn't the first time I'd noticed Stan go out of his way for Philip. On our field trip to the winery he'd given up his seat in the back of the van so Philip wouldn't have to sit shotgun. (Of course Stan had talked the driver's ear off all the way to Clos d'Été.) Then just the day before, I'd seen Stan gingerly adjust Philip's crooked toque. It seemed while I was fixated on Luc, my friend was developing his own crush. I made a mental note to interrogate him about it later, but at the moment, I had a new crisis on my hands. My rescued hollandaise wouldn't keep for long. I had to work fast to poach my eggs. A heavy pot of water was boiling on the back burner. Buttered, toasted English muffin slices topped with thick slabs of Canadian bacon were already waiting on plates. All I had to do was poach five perfect eggs—one for each judge and Stefan and one that the production assistants would take away for photography. Easier said than done.

Chef Bouchard cut into his egg—my egg—and as I'd hoped, the yolk spilled out, a bright orange-yellow puddle seeping across the plate. He speared a piece of egg white and ham on English muffin and swirled the whole bite through the runny yolk and hollandaise sauce.

After swallowing, he said, "Sophie, I am very impressed

with your poached egg. It looks like a professional chef's." He lifted the edge of the egg with his fork, examining it as a doctor would a patient. "Your hollandaise is a little thin though quite good. . . ." No whammy, no whammy, I thought. "But," he continued—dang it—"it doesn't show much originality."

"This dish just didn't do it for me," Patricia said. "I could have gotten it in any restaurant—any good restaurant, I should say. It was fine, but it was just that. It felt like you were just going through the motions."

I was! I wanted to shout. The motions Chef Bouchard taught me this week!

"But your eggs were nicely cooked," Patricia offered as consolation. "Tommy, what did you think of the presentation?"

"A garnish would have been nice for some color. Chive or parsley?"

I nodded, but inside I was steaming. The week before I'd been hammered for messing with a classic. Now they were telling me my dish was too classic. What did these people want from me?

Evidently they wanted perfection, because that was how they described Shelby's mussels in garlic cream sauce. After forty-five minutes of deliberation, during which time we were sent to the locker room beside the kitchen to stew, the judges announced her as the winner. In second place were Britney's peach crepes with crème fraîche, which elicited a tightened jaw but not much else from Dante, who'd had to resort to apricots; and in third, despite my lack of originality, my eggs Benedict.

Shelby beamed when Tommy declared her at the top of the class. She all but curtsied when he presented the set of Japanese knives she'd won.

While I was excited for my friend and proud of her, of course, there was a little part of me that couldn't help but be annoyed at her unwavering confidence. Just a little insecurity would have gone a long way. As it was, Shelby wasn't exactly winning any Miss Congeniality contests. I loved her, but it was no coincidence she'd butted heads with several contestants.

"Cut!" the MIB suddenly yelled. He'd been watching from the periphery of the room. We all turned, no one with as startled a look on her face as Shelby.

"Sorry, guys," he said, walking onto the set. It was the first time he had interrupted filming. His direction normally came before the cameras rolled in the form of reminders not to look directly into the lens or to speak up. Occasionally he placed us in a "scene" so that no one's back was to the cameras or they had a better sight line. But he had never just yelled "cut." It was a jarring reminder that this was all for the folks at home.

"Marcus," the MIB snapped at onc of the cameramen standing behind the judges' table, "your view is blocked by Patricia's head. Come on."

I felt a twinge of satisfaction as Patricia and her big head blushed. She self-consciously tucked a stray hair behind her ear.

"Sorry, Pete," the cameraman said and readjusted between Chef Bouchard and Stefan, who sat at the end of the table. I wondered if Stefan was jealous he wasn't a real judge. It certainly would have explained his bad attitude.

"All right, Shelby," the MIB said. Shelby, for the first time I'd ever seen, looked unsure. "We're gonna take that again from Tommy's announcement that you're the winner. I'd like you to do exactly what you just did. You were great, fantastic. We just want to make sure you have your moment."

"No problem," Shelby said, her composure suddenly back full force.

"Excellent." The MIB receded back to the shadows. "Still rolling!"

Week 3

ASIAN CUISINE

Chapter Eight

A tear slid from the corner of my eye to my pillow. I didn't like this pillow. The pillowcase was nubbier than my pillow at home. It rubbed against my cheek when I lay on my side. So I was on my back, staring at the bottom of Shelby's top bunk. When I should have been resting for the next morning's test.

When the eight of us had come back to the dorm that night after dinner, there had been a mysterious red stock-pot in the middle of the common room coffee table. Fearing some sort of twist, we'd elected Dante to look under the lid. Inside were not blindfolds or instructions for a surprise challenge but postcards from our families. The photo on mine was of the Washington Monument during the Cherry Blossom Festival, my favorite time of year in DC. My eyes welled with tears as I read the handwritten note on the back:

Sophia—We love you and miss you!

Buona fortuna!

It was signed by Baba, Nonna, Pappou, Raffi, and Alex. My heart stopped. Alex had signed it. Did that mean something? Did Alex *miss* me? Did he *love* me, like the postcard said?

I tossed and turned in bed for hours trying to decode the meaning of the postcard and what should be two simple words. I had been in California for two weeks and five days. I had talked to my father five times, seen my aunt once, and had no contact with Alex until now. I even missed my brother. Maybe my homesickness was making me read too much into things, I told myself.

I needed to sleep. The theme that week was Asian cuisine. We were working with things like tofu and Chinese five-spice powder and fish sauce—flavors and ingredients totally out of my comfort zone. Also, it was finally happening—what was bound to happen and what happened on every reality show: We were cracking under the pressure. Ingredients for the afternoon labs were, mysteriously, becoming more scarce, and Stefan wasn't sending anyone down to the storeroom for more. When we complained that there wasn't enough lemongrass or that we were out of ginger, Stefan merely shrugged and told us to "think like chefs." So we scrambled to claim what we needed to complete our recipes, suspiciously eyeing the others to make sure they weren't stockpiling in an effort to sabotage the rest of us.

The kitchen even felt smaller than it had the first two

weeks, although I knew that was impossible. On Tuesday, Britney freaked when Philip turned quickly with a hot sauté pan, almost burning her. Then on Wednesday, Mario had blamed Maura for moving his salmon from the walk-in fridge. When confronted, she denied it, but no one else would own up. Maura had already cried four times that week, twice in one day after Stefan berated her for not listening and then questioned her commitment to learning anything here on *Teen Test Kitchen*. I'd even watched Dante warn a cameraman to get out of his face. We were losing it. And we still had four more weeks. Four more weeks without our families and without our best friends, who weren't helping things by sending confusing postcards.

I finally drifted off to sleep around two A.M., five hours before I had to be up again. I dreamed that I was hosting a cooking show. Stefan was there, and Chef Bouchard and Patricia. Tommy, true to life, wasn't. Shelby and Stan and my mother were in the audience. My father was the cameraman. Everyone expected me to make a dish, but no one would tell me what it was, so I'd throw ingredients in a bowl and watch for their reaction. At one point, I asked my father for help, but he just smiled. He couldn't hear me; I was on my own.

"Your time is up," Stefan snapped.

Three red zeros flashed on the giant timer on the wall. I rotated the handle of the ceramic spoon holding my plum dipping sauce so that it faced the same direction as the spoons on my three other plates. The sauce was way too sweet, but it was all I had.

"Done!" I raised my hands above my head like the others. Britney gave me a dirty look.

My presentation was appealing, the components lined neatly on white rectangular plates, but I could have told you right then that my Wontons Three Ways were no winners. The first wonton was wrapped like a mini spring roll around glass noodles, carrots, and shredded cabbage and accompanied by the plum sauce. The second was a savory dumpling filled with a mixture of ground pork, green onions, and spices. I'd drizzled it with an orange juice and soy reduction. The third wonton was an experiment: I'd fried sliced wonton wrappers and drizzled them with honey and powdered sugar. A grand idea, but looking at my plates, I knew my three pieces just didn't go together. I should have done Wontons One Way. The week before, I'd wanted first place and gotten third. This time I would have been happy not to wind up at the bottom of the class.

Tommy appreciated my increased attention to plating, but the fact that I'd had to make it look good because it didn't taste good didn't escape anyone. Chef Bouchard called my flavor profiles "way off," and Patricia asked if I had tasted my dish, to which I sheepishly nodded yes.

What was I doing here? I wondered for the millionth time as they picked apart my dish bite by bite. My culinary career was deflating like a fallen soufflé before my eyes. Why would Tommy Chang want an apprentice who couldn't even make a decent egg roll?

While I was slowly dying of shame, it seemed the showdown would be between Philip's bibimbap, a Korean dish I couldn't pronounce let alone cook, and Stan's Indian chicken tikka masala with cucumber raita, both of which the judges loved. Philip's giant bowls contained everything but the kitchen sink: rice, five different vegetables, a red paste, something that looked like kelp, beef, and a semiraw egg. It looked like a jumble to me. In fact, the only person who didn't seem upset when Tommy announced Philip as thc winner was, surprisingly, Stan.

"Congratulations," Stan said, hugging Philip once the cameras had stopped rolling. Philip blushed. By now, everyone knew they were an item, but Philip was still somehow under the impression that their romance was a secret.

Shelby and I stood off to the side. "If I'd known raw eggs were the trick," I said out of the corner of my mouth, "I wouldn't have spent so much time poaching the damn things last week."

Shelby's arms were crossed tightly. I could practically see the steam coming off her in waves. But she was annoyed this time with Stan, not Philip. "It's ridiculous," she said. "Stan's so hot and bothered for Philip, he doesn't even care. I mean look at him!"

She motioned over at the two boys just as Stan glanced at us. One of his bushy eyebrows jutted upward. He sensed her pique. "Can I help you, Shel?"

Uh-oh . . .

"You know, sometimes I wonder if you even want this, Stan," Shelby snapped. "Is this all just a game to you?"

"It is a game," Stan said.

"Not for some of us."

"If this is all so important to you, if cooking is 'your life,'" Stan said, making mocking air quotes, "then how come you can't even bring yourself to taste the food you make, Shelby?"

Stefan, Patricia, and Chef Bouchard were talking with the MIB in the corner. At the uneasy silence that had suddenly engulfed the room, they all turned. The MIB gestured quickly toward a cameraman, who hefted his equipment to his shoulder just in time to catch Shelby storm out of the kitchen.

"What was that?" I asked Stan.

"What?" he said defensively. "We all know." But he looked sorry.

The truth was it hadn't escaped me, or anyone else I suspected, that Shelby rarely ate the dishes she made, or food period. She was more likely to push it around on her plate. "No artist likes her own art," she'd joke, but even when we tried each others' dishes in labs, she took only the tiniest bite. Several times I'd caught her reading the nutrition information on the back of the snacks at the craft service table, adding up calories and carbs in her head. I could probably stand to do more of that—certainly Stan could, but Shelby was already beanpole thin. Where my ample Mediterranean booty knocked around the kitchen, hers disappeared under the baggy folds of her uniform. Her body was all angles, although all she ever talked about was food. It was as if her obsession had taken all the pleasure out of it. Maybe, I decided, if I could show her how to enjoy it again, I could get Team S back on track.

"Okay," I said later that night after a very awkward dinner. Stan had sat with Philip while Shelby and I dined silently at our table, Shelby picking self-consciously at her penne with braised short ribs.

Somehow I had coaxed them into meeting on the dorm patio, although neither of them would look at the other. It was obvious for the survival of Team S that I would have to play peacemaker. I persevered. "Tomorrow we have the day off, and I know what we're going to do."

"I hope it doesn't involve cooking," Stan muttered.

"Not quite," I said. "But probably watching people cook. And maybe eating. I want to take you guys to my aunt's restaurant."

"Do you think they'll let us?" Stan asked.

Shelby was still obstinately quiet.

"They let me. The restaurant is awesome, and my aunt knows everything about anything grown, raised, or eaten in Napa. She buys her ingredients fresh every day. She has this amazing herb garden in giant tubs—Stan, you'd like it; you could do it in New York."

Neither Shelby nor Stan said anything. They both stared in different directions.

"All right," I said, standing. "I'm glad we're in agreement. See you at eleven. This Wrongton Wonder is going to bed."

The producers let us go but insisted we take a van this time. The cameraman climbed in with us. Stan and Shelby had said nothing at breakfast about their fight, but before I'd gone to bed, I'd peeked through the window to see them still sitting across from each other at the patio table. I wasn't sure who'd apologized first, but I had a feeling it wasn't Shelby.

"The Last Supper?" the driver asked.

"The Last Supper?" repeated Stan. "That's a bit morbid, isn't it?"

"It's kind of nice, actually—my aunt says you should enjoy every meal as if it were your last."

"I like it," Shelby decided.

"Very tortured and existential," said Stan.

I laughed. "Actually, she's not like that at all. She's kind of a hippie. You can tell she really believes in what she's doing."

"Saving the world one succotash at a time," said Stan.

"Something like that."

And in a very freaky coincidence, herbed summer succotash was on the day's menu. Aunt Mary was test driving several new recipes that she wanted us to try. Shelby, Stan, and I stood mesmerized around the large butcher block table in the center of the Last Supper kitchen as my aunt deftly handled her ingredients. Chanterelle mushrooms and bunches of fragrant basil and arugula lay on the table. A pan was warming behind her, waiting for a pile of tender Pacific scallops. One of the biggest mistakes new chefs make, Chef Bouchard had taught us, was to start with a cold pan. Your cooking surface should be hot before the food hits it. Aunt Mary held her hand above the pan to gauge the temperature.

"So you really worked at Chez Panisse?" Shelby asked.

"I did," Aunt Mary said. "I learned a lot there."

"Like what?" I asked, remembering how Luc had talked of the restaurant that day in the root cellar.

"Well, that you have to respect your ingredients, first and foremost. I don't plan my menus until I've seen and tasted the ingredients. They'll tell you what to make."

“Wow,” Stan murmured. “That’s so Zen.”

Aunt Mary laughed. “Is it? I wish everyone could eat that way. It’s crazy how we feed ourselves these days—importing tomatoes in December and frozen fish from Iceland when we have all this bounty in our own backyard. Don’t even get me started on the preservatives and steroids and genetic modification. Did you know there are thirty-eight ingredients in a Chicken McNugget? Thirty-eight! And thirteen of those are derived from corn.”

Aunt Mary tossed some minced shallots into the heated oil, where they sizzled. She dashed in some white wine and shook the pan vigorously. “Your grandmother wouldn’t recognize half of what we eat today as food,” she said to me.

I knew she meant her mother—my mom’s mother, not Nonna. I hadn’t known her either. Grandma and Grandpa Harris had died the year I was born.

“Did she teach you to cook?” I asked, jealous of the idea of having a mother around to do such things.

“Your grandmother? No, she couldn’t boil water. She taught me to garden, though.” My aunt had walked Shelby and Stan through the restaurant’s garden, identifying each vegetable and herb and her favorite dishes to make with them. “Your mom was the one who got me into cooking.”

A sudden pang clawed at my stomach. I told myself it was just hunger. At least I knew how to cure that.

And sure enough, an hour later, I could barely recall what hunger had ever felt like. The meal Aunt Mary prepared was impeccable. We’d feasted on goat cheese and chanterelle crostini and pan-seared scallops over herbed summer succotash. Even Shelby had all but licked her plate clean.

"You can't be full yet, Stanley! There's still dessert," my aunt teased.

Stan rubbed his belly. "I couldn't possibly. I ate enough food to feed the village."

"You mean *a* village," I corrected.

"No," Stan said. "I meant *the* Village."

"Sophie," Shelby said, a gleam coming to her eye, "you should have invited Luc!"

"Luc Renault?" Aunt Mary asked.

Red-faced, I nodded and pleaded with my eyes for my aunt not to say anything more in front of the cameraman. I didn't want him reporting back to the producers.

"He's cute," my aunt said approvingly.

"Tell me about it," Stan and Shelby said at the same time. "Jinx!" they both yelled.

Aunt Mary cocked her head, reading my silent entreaty for her to stay mum. "Maybe next time," she said and dropped it. I was grateful.

The telephone cord curled around my finger. The closetlike room where we made our calls home was wallpapered in old covers of *Foodie* magazine. It contained a beanbag chair, a retro rotary phone, and of course, a surveillance camera.

My relief at hearing my father's voice was quickly turning to the more typical exasperation. He had just told me Aunt Mary's restaurant sounded "frou-frou."

"Dad," I insisted, "it's not frou-frou. It's just fresh, good food."

"Bah. We make fresh, good food here! How is it so different?"

"I don't know," I said. "It just is. She grows her own ingredients and knows where her eggs come from."

"I know where my eggs come from."

"Sysco doesn't count, Dad."

"Don't get smart, Sophia. I'm glad that you're spending time with your aunt. And I'm glad that you like her restaurant so much. So what are you learning?"

"We had our Asian cuisine test on Friday. I made wontons three ways."

"One wasn't enough?"

"Three apparently wasn't enough."

"What? Those people serve a pea on a plate and call it cuisine."

"No, they don't, Dad. They just don't pile a pound of pasta on a plate."

"I was watching one of those foodie shows the other night, and a guy was cooking with liquid nitrogen. Nitrogen! He made bacon ice cream with egg foam! Called it molecular gastrology."

"Molecular gastronomy."

"Whatever it is, I can't believe it! Food, Sophia, food . . ." He liked to accentuate his points by repeating himself. I leaned back in the beanbag chair, already knowing by heart the lecture I was about to hear. "Is about sharing a meal. It's about gathering around the table with your family and friends."

I could imagine my father gesticulating wildly in our kitchen, becoming increasingly animated as the rant went on. "It's about community, not chemicals and crazy machines!"

"Is that what you think I'm learning here?" I asked.

"I don't know. Is it?"

I was pissed now. All this hard work, and he still didn't understand. "Dad, you'll never know what it means to be a real chef. I don't want to make lasagna for the rest of my life."

"Would that be so bad?" I didn't answer, and his voice got calmer. "Sophia, I just don't want you to get wrapped up in the glamour and the fads. Remember who you are, where you come from."

"You're right, Dad," I said, sliding forward on the beanbag's Styrofoam pellets. I was starting to get a headache. "You know, I really should go. I have more fads to learn this week."

"Sophia."

I knew better than to hang up on my father. "Bye, Dad. My ten minutes are up. I have to go."

"Good-bye, Sophia. I love you," he was saying as I lowered the receiver onto its red plastic cradle.

I laid my head in my hands. Maybe my father was right. Maybe the glamour of being a top chef wasn't for me. Not because I didn't want it, but because I couldn't hack it. A knock at the door startled me. It cracked open to reveal Megan, the assistant producer. "Hey," she said. "We need to tape your Kitchen Confidential."

"Dang it, I forgot."

"Yeah. Sorry. Peter's waiting for you in the Box."

"The Box" was what we'd started calling the room where we filmed our video diaries. "Okay," I sighed. "I'll be right there."

Dragging myself from the beanbag chair, I made my way down the hall to a door with a paper sign taped to it that read QUIET—FILMING IN PROGRESS.

I knocked. The MIB greeted me with a smile. "Hello, Sophie."

I took my place in front of yet another camera.

After a few stale lead-in questions, the MIB surprised me by asking, "Would you ever want to run your family's restaurant?"

There it was. It was almost as if he'd been listening in on my conversation—or my life. This was the question that had quietly lurked in the background of my relationship with my father for years. I knew, without him having to say it, that my father saw the matter differently: Did I think I was too good for the life he'd built? Of course, that wasn't how I saw it at all.

"No," I answered the MIB's question matter-of-factly. I'd never said it out loud before.

Peter stopped playing with the pen he was twirling between his fingers. "Why not?" he asked.

I thought about it. I hadn't come to Napa because I wanted to be a reality star. I hadn't even really come for the apprenticeship with Tommy Chang or the scholarship, though I certainly wouldn't turn them down. No, I had flown across the country, thousands of miles from my family and my best friend, and put myself at the mercy of producers and a panel of judges who seemed to enjoy squashing my dreams, because I wanted to learn something, because I wanted to see what I was capable of, because, to borrow from Uncle Sam, I wanted to be all that I could be. And what I could be was more than the chef at Taverna Ristorante. So how could I answer the MIB's question?

"I can make manicotti blindfolded," I replied. "I've been a cook. I came here to be a chef."

Peter smiled. "Great!" he said, standing up. "Good Confidential, Sophie. See you tomorrow."

"That's it?" I asked.

"Yep." He pushed a button on the camera mounted on a tripod behind his chair. "That's it. We got what we need."

Aunt Mary's Summer Succotash

Aunt Mary calls this dish "summer on a plate." Succotash (funny name, serious taste) shows how fresh, in-season produce needs just the least amount of cooking to bring out its flavors. She makes it only in the summer, when she can go to the farmers' market and find the best and ripest vegetables herself. The rest of the year, we wait for summer so we can make it again.

SERVES 4 as a side dish

Ingredients

1 tablespoon extra-virgin olive oil
1 thick slice bacon, finely diced
3 shallots, minced
3 medium tomatoes, peeled, seeded, and coarsely chopped
2 cups fresh lima beans, boiled until tender
3 ears corn, kernels cut off
Kosher salt and freshly ground pepper to taste
2 tablespoons unsalted butter
¼ cup chopped basil leaves

Directions

1. Heat olive oil in a large skillet. Add bacon and cook over moderately high heat until browned. Add shallots and cook until just softened.

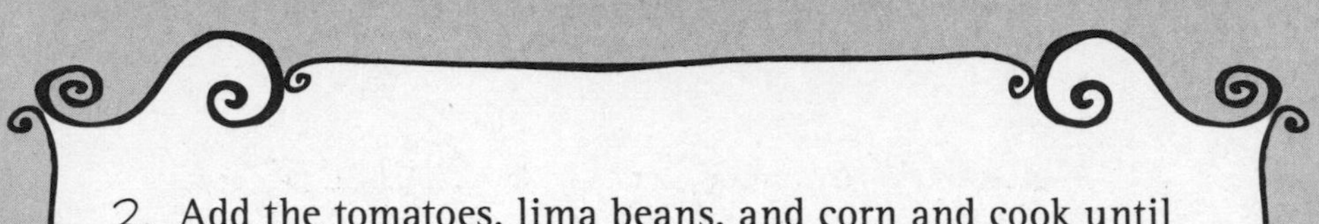

2. Add the tomatoes, lima beans, and corn and cook until the tomatoes break down, about 10 minutes. Season with salt and pepper. Stir in the butter and basil, and serve.

Week 4

MEDITERRANEAN CUISINE

Chapter Nine

Of course after my big talk of blindfolded manicotti making, the week's theme was Mediterranean. We'd be studying Italian, Greek, and some Middle Eastern food. It was finally my chance to shine. These flavors were in my blood.

We cranked pappardelle and crimped ravioli. We rolled ropes of potato gnocchi. Stan watched with awe as I churned out perfect, equal pockets of ricotta-stuffed goodness. But pasta is nothing without its sauce, so on the second day we were learning a creamy gorgonzola-walnut sauce and a traditional marinara.

"Is someone using this cutting board?" Mario asked.

"I am," Philip replied from across the room, where he was sautéing onions and garlic.

Mario grumbled. "Can I use this one then?"

"No, I'm using that one," Britney said.

Mario moved on in search of another board.

The kitchen was chaotic, as usual. So I might have expected some splatter. What I didn't expect was for the saucepot of marinara that Dante was carrying to collide with me and empty its entire contents down the front of my white uniform.

"Crap!" Dante said, mopping at my jacket with a nearby towel. "Sorry, Sophie."

"Are you okay?" Maura shrieked after turning to see my front covered in blood-red liquid.

"It's just sauce," I replied, nevertheless annoyed.

Stan laughed. "You look like Carrie!" He picked up a butcher knife and made horror movie stabbing motions in my direction.

"What's going on?" Stefan was beside us in an instant.

"I spilled my marinara on her," Dante explained. I turned to show Stefan the sauce dripping like a Rorschach blot down the front of my jacket.

"So I see." Stefan's lip curled. "Well, you'll have to change."

The first rule of the Test Kitchen was that our uniforms had to be clean. Any chef worth his or her salt keeps his jacket a shade of blinding white that is meant to signify cleanliness.

"What about my sauce?" I asked. "I just started simmering the tomatoes."

Stefan ignored my question. "Where is your extra uniform?"

We all had a spare we'd been issued the first day. Most people kept theirs in the locker room. Unfortunately, this was my spare. My other uniform already had soy sauce on it from Friday and was back in our room awaiting a PA to come for laundry. "Well . . ." My gaze fell to the floor.

"You'll have to borrow one," Stefan ordered.

"You can borrow mine," Shelby called from her stovetop.

"Thanks."

In the locker room, I found Shelby's spare jacket on a hanger and felt on the shelf for the folded pants. As I pulled them down, something else dropped to the ground with them. It was a notebook, the kind of marbled composition book we used in elementary school. I knelt to pick it up. It had fallen open to a handwritten page. BRITNEY GIBSON it said at the top, all caps and underlined. Below were notes about Britney's age and hometown. Printed out and taped to the next page was a newspaper article about Britney's winning the Southern California *Teen Test Kitchen* qualifier. In the margins were more notes, these more subjective. "Terrible knife skills," said one. Another, "Creative plating—keep an eye on."

A memory clicked. Our first night in Napa, Shelby had told Stan and me about a notebook with information on all the winners of the regional casting competitions. But she'd said the producers confiscated it. Had she been lying? Had she been keeping it this whole time?

I flipped past Dante's name and Maura's, past a page on a girl named Rebecca with a question mark, apparently a false lead, and found mine. SOPHIE NICOLAIDES it said at the top of the page. "Greek? 16, Washington, DC. Taverna Ristorante—Italian?"

I knew the local TV news report she'd gotten the information from. Alex had e-mailed it to me, and even Nonna and Pappou had crowded around the computer to watch the video.

But it was what I read next that made my blood boil. There were two neat columns in precise, type-A handwriting:

Strengths	Weaknesses
Mediterranean flavors	Sloppy plating
Timing/multitasking	Overseasoning
	Unsophisticated

Unsophisticated. I zeroed in on the word. Me, or my food? How could Shelby write this about me, about all of us? How could she lie to me and Stan? What about Team S? If there ever was a Team S, I suddenly thought. What was her game? What was she saying behind my back? Was she bashing me like this in her Kitchen Confidentials? My cheeks burned.

I threw on the clean jacket and tucked the book into the waist of my pants. I had to get back to the kitchen. If my work was so sloppy and unsophisticated, I supposed I couldn't stand to miss a class, even one on Mediterranean flavors.

The lab didn't last long. Shortly after I returned to the kitchen, Patricia appeared. We were taking a surprise field trip to the farmers' market.

It wasn't quite as busy as the day I'd gone with Aunt Mary, but the market was still thronged with tourists and local foodies. Our flock of teenagers wearing chef's whites and trailed by a camera crew was getting plenty of attention. We followed Patricia as she moved from stand to stand, encouraging us to taste samples and ask the farmers questions.

At one point, Shelby sidled up to me. "Love the jacket," she joked. "Where'd you get it?"

"Your locker," I answered humorlessly. I popped an organic cherry tomato into my mouth. The words from the notebook still burned in my mind. That's what it was—a burn book.

"I know. I was kidding. I can't believe Dante spilled sauce all over you."

"Yeah."

"Are you okay?" Shelby eyed me quizzically.

"Why wouldn't I be?"

I separated myself from Shelby. I wasn't ready to confront her yet about the notebook, not on camera and especially not in front of Patricia, who was gathering us around a new stall. It was one Aunt Mary and I had visited.

"This is the best sheep's milk ricotta," I said, taking one of their little plastic tasting spoons. The cheese was smooth and creamy with just the slightest tang.

Patricia looked surprised. "It is! You've had it before?"

"Once," I replied. "There's another stand around here with sage that my aunt mixes with this ricotta for ravioli. Brown-something Herb Farm?"

"Brown Nose Herb Farm?" Britney said under her breath. Maura tittered.

Patricia didn't hear them. "Brown Bear Herb Farm," she said. "It's a good one. You know your way around, Sophie!" It was probably the first time I'd seen a smile on her face.

"You do," Stefan agreed, with a hint of suspicion I couldn't help but notice.

"My aunt showed me around."

"When you saw her last week?" Mario asked. I hadn't realized he was also listening.

"No, the first weekend. When you all went into St. Helena."

"How nice—a personal tour," Philip said sarcastically.

Why did I suddenly feel as if everyone was ganging up on me? First Shelby and now this? The producers had given me permission to see my aunt. It wasn't as if I'd smuggled recipes back to the set. Why was I suddenly the bad guy? Shelby, innocently chatting with Stan like he was her BFF, was the one who'd backstabbed us all.

When we got back to school, I proceeded straight up to our room. Shelby followed me. "Sophie, are you sure everything's okay?" she asked, closing the door behind us for some semblance of privacy.

I spun around. "No," I answered now that the cameras weren't around. I knew they—the ever-present, ominous they—could still hear us on our wireless mics, but I didn't care anymore. "It's not okay."

"O-kay," Shelby said, drawing out the letters, "then what's wrong?"

Did she really think the clueless act would work? She had to know she'd be found out sometime. Burn books are always found.

"What's wrong is that you think I'm 'unsophisticated' and 'sloppy.' Were you ever really my friend? Or were you just getting close to me so you could pick me apart, know my weaknesses?"

Shelby reeled back, looking genuinely shocked at the hurt and anger in my voice. "What are you talking about?"

"The notebook."

"What notebook?"

"The one in your locker." Shelby appeared baffled. "Your 'competition research.'"

"The one they took from me when I got here?" she asked. Her face still held its dubious mask of confusion.

"Maybe you're missing your calling. Maybe you should be a food critic," I said.

Shelby's expression changed as she shifted from defense to offense. "What are you saying, Sophie?"

"You certainly have some strong opinions. I guess I do overseason on occasion. I didn't realize you were planning on using it against me, though. I thought we were in this together. What was all that Team S crap? Does Stan know?"

Shelby's gray eyes flashed with indignation. "Does Stan know what? Sophie, I told you about the notebook. It wasn't a big deal. I did research on my competition. So what? I haven't seen it since we got here."

"Whatever, Shelby."

"Yeah, whatever, Sophie."

I slammed the door to our room behind me as a production assistant in the hall whispered urgently into her headset.

Later that night, Shelby and I had simmered down thanks only to the mediation skills of Stan. "My parents have had me in psychotherapy since I was five," he'd assured us as he ushered us both back to our room after dinner once the mics were off. I wasn't sure yet whether I wanted the producers to know about the burn book. After all, it said some less than flattering things about me. Confronting Shelby while still mic'ed earlier had been stupid.

Shelby swore up and down, on her future college

acceptance, that the notebook had been hers but that it had been confiscated like she'd said. She hadn't seen it, much less made new notes in it, since she'd gotten to Napa.

"Then why is everyone but you in it?" I asked.

"I don't know. Look, I don't have time to focus on anyone else," she insisted. "I'm just trying to get my own dishes out. Besides, I'd never write those things about you guys. You're both extremely talented chefs. Stan, I told you just the other day how good your vindaloo was."

I wasn't sold yet on her innocence, which I communicated with my silence. Stan, however, seemed to believe her. "Something is definitely rotten in the state of Denmark," he said as he flipped through the offending pages.

Shelby and I read over his shoulder. "Dang!" Stan would remark occasionally at some comment that was particularly harsh, like the word *airhead* printed next to Maura's name or his own characterization as an "unfocused fluffball."

"*That*'s not my handwriting!" Shelby protested.

"Well," Stan finally said. He closed the book and set it on the bottom bunk beside him, clasping his hands around his knees. "I don't think the writing is Shelby's. At least not the inarticulate and misinformed swill that's been written since we got here."

"See?" Shelby said, throwing up her hands. "Thank you, Stanley."

"The ink of the later writing is a slightly different shade of blue. More cerulean, if you will, than the ultramarine of the earlier writing." Stan folded over a page of the notebook paper to compare the two ink colors. He was right.

"So maybe the writer used a different blue pen." I

avoided saying maybe *Shelby* had used a different blue pen.

"The lowercase *a*'s are a little different, too. See?" Stan pointed to the words *laughable* and *California*. Indeed, the *a*'s of the first word had more of a tail. "And there's more weight on the tip of the pen with the really mean notes."

"Did you study handwriting at the police academy, Detective Goldberg?" Shelby's sense of humor seemed to be back now that she felt cleared of the charges.

"I am one of New York's finest," said Stan. "And I did have to forge several signatures to get out of gym."

Actually, I felt relieved at Stan's conclusion. I hadn't wanted those thoughts to be Shelby's. Her friendship had become important to me. She looked at me expectantly, her arms folded over her chest.

"I'm sorry, Shelby," I said. For a second I wondered if she'd forgive me. "I shouldn't have doubted you."

"It's all right," she finally said. "This show's making us all crazy."

"But if you didn't write that stuff," Stan said, voicing what we were all thinking, "then who did?"

"And how and why did the notebook suddenly reappear in *my* locker?" Shelby asked. "Why did someone want me to see it?"

"Those," I said, gnawing my nails to stubs as we all stared at the mysterious notebook, "are the burning questions of the burn book."

Chapter Ten

We had a short breather after lunch before our Mediterranean test. Stan and Shelby went back to the dorm, but I wanted to enjoy the sun on the cafeteria patio. The crew was holding a meeting in the corner. I was still deciding what dish to make in less than an hour. This week was mine—as long as I didn't screw it up. The judges had blasted me for messing with the classics, then complained that my dishes weren't showing my personality. They seemed to want me to embrace my background, but I could hardly make manicotti after my brilliant comments in the Kitchen Confidential. Maybe something Greek? I knew most of the others would be focusing on Italian. But I was torn between spanakopita, a savory pastry stuffed with spinach and feta, and a favorite of mine, and youvetsi, a rustic lamb dish baked with orzo in a tomato sauce. The scrape of a metal chair on brick interrupted my deliberation. To my happy surprise, it was Luc. I hadn't seen him around campus in almost two weeks, since our meeting in the cellar.

"May I sit?" he asked, waiting for me to say "of course" before pulling a chair to the table. "How is it going?"

"Fine," I sighed.

His expression became gravely serious. "Ah. 'Fine.' I know whenever an American girl says 'fine' she is lying."

"Oh, do you know that about American girls?" I teased.

"You look like something is on your mind," he pressed. "The other day I saw you across campus. You were—how do you say?—scowling." He did a pretty cute imitation of my pissed-off face—"the stormy Greek," Alex called it.

There was something on my mind. A lot, actually. Beyond my test in an hour, the puzzle of the burn book was still gnawing at me. Shelby, Stan, and I, after hours of looking for clues in the book itself, still had no idea who was behind it. It had to be one of the others, but how had the notebook escaped the producers' hands? And why had the co-author wanted it back in Shelby's possession? Furthermore, why had he (or she) not added anything about Shelby and insulted himself? To disguise his identity, we guessed. Still, we had more questions than answers.

That Luc had watched me from across campus, and closely enough to register my mood, flattered me. But I hesitated to tell him about the burn book, afraid it might seem petty to him. "Was it on Tuesday you saw me?" I asked, recalling my foul mood after finding the notebook.

Luc frowned as he thought. "No. It was Saturday. I had just come back from Clos d'Été."

I loved how the name of the winery sounded almost musical on his lips. Those perfect lips . . . Focus. I thought back to Saturday, the day we'd been to Aunt Mary's. But I'd been in a good mood that night . . . until I talked to my father. I remembered our argument and how annoyed I'd been that our short phone time was wasted on it.

I nodded guiltily. "Yeah. I kind of got in a fight with my dad on the phone."

Luc murmured sympathetically.

"I shouldn't have gotten mad at him. He's the reason I am a chef. He taught me everything. But he has this way of, I don't know, pushing my buttons. He doesn't get it, you know? He doesn't get why I'm here. He knows it's a big deal. But he thinks it's only a phase, that I'll come home and end up working in our restaurant just like him."

"Ah." Luc nodded knowingly. He folded his hands on the table in front of him. "Yes, I know that problem well."

"Your dad? He owns a winery! How could he not get this?" I waved my hands at everything around us: the culinary academy, the bountiful landscape, the foodie culture and the incredible chefs and restaurants that came out of it, and most important, the basic belief that food can be art.

"No," Luc said. "Not my father. My mother."

"The one in Paris?"

"Yes."

"But she's in Paris! That's, like, the land of good food! You guys invented it."

Luc laughed. "Yes, we mostly have a different attitude

about food than you do here, but not everyone in Paris is as . . . enlightened as you and me." He grinned.

"She's a businesswoman," Luc continued. "She thinks what my father does is not serious, a hobby."

"He's one of the best vintners in Napa! He's won awards."

"Yes," he granted. "So have I. But it's not in her blood." He shrugged. "What about your mother? Does she also want you to come home and work in the restaurant?"

Again it had arrived: the moment in every new relationship—if you were so inclined to stretch the meaning of the word in this instance—when I had to explain. "My mother's not around," I said.

"Oh. I'm sorry," he replied but didn't press any further. "And why would working in your father's restaurant be so bad?"

"It wouldn't be bad, just . . ." I realized the production meeting had broken up. "Sorry," I said quickly. "Camera's coming."

Luc glanced over at the cameraman casually approaching our table. He sat up straight. "Yes," he said as the guy lifted his camera to his shoulder, "I think it would be wise to take a pastry course."

"A pastry course," I said, nodding intently. "I suppose every chef should know the basics of pastry. There's so much to learn: cakes, pies, tarts, custards . . ."

"Brioche, puff pastry, croissants. Not to mention the cookies," he added.

"And meringues."

"Of course meringues."

The cameraman pretended to film the landscape behind

us, one he'd shot two hundred times before. Very stealthy. But it seemed our strategy was working. When I asked Luc about his food safety class, the cameraman unshouldered his camera and wandered back into the cafeteria. We were boring.

"Thanks," I said.

Luc feigned confusion. "I thought you really wanted to know about the pastry course." I laughed. He leaned in closer. "I have an idea," he whispered.

"About pastry?"

"No. An adventure."

My heart flittered. "What kind of adventure?"

"Do you trust me?" he asked.

"Do I trust you? I don't know you!"

He stuck out his hand. "Hello. I'm Luc, the dashing French culinary student you met on a reality show in California. What's not to trust?" He smiled wickedly. He had so many smiles, I couldn't keep up with them all.

"True," I conceded.

"Tomorrow is Saturday. You have it free, yes?"

"Yes."

Luc grabbed the pen and paper I'd been doodling my recipe ideas on and scribbled something. He turned it to me so I could read it: *Do you know where the loading dock is?* I nodded, suddenly remembering my microphone. I was getting used to it now—too used to it. Luc didn't want whoever was on the listening end to hear what he was about to propose.

We never had reason to go to the loading dock behind the school, but we'd seen it on our tour of the NCA campus our first day. It was not a very romantic place, but for a rendezvous point, it was perfect—quiet on a Saturday and out of view.

He wrote upside down on the paper: 10 AM. "If you trust me," he said aloud. "If you don't, no offense."

"Okay," I answered before I knew what I was saying.

Luc didn't ask if that meant "okay, I'll be there," or "okay, I'll consider." He just smiled, yet another dazzler.

"One more question," I said before he walked away. "Spanakopita or youvetsi?"

"Spanakopita," he said without hesitation.

A boy after my own heart.

I went with spanakopita. Because I had extra time, I also made an arugula salad with lemon-garlic vinaigrette. It was simple but delicious, not too wild but acceptably "ethnic" and, hopefully, what the judges were looking for. Philip had won the Asian test with his Korean bibimpap. Now everyone was watching the Greek girl for her spanakopita.

After presenting to the judges, we were sent to the locker room while they deliberated. It was torture. We'd started calling it the Pressure Cooker. Their decision could take ten minutes or an hour. Or they could just enjoy seeing us sweat. I settled in for the wait with my back against one of the lockers.

"Your fettuccine looked awesome," Mario told Britney.

Britney's handmade fettuccine with asparagus, pine nuts, and shaved Parmesan did, indeed, look awesome. The burn book was right in this case—her plates, no matter how they tasted, always looked like a work of art. It was obvious she was one of Tommy's favorites. But Britney was less sure of herself. "I don't know," she worried. "The pasta was kind of difficult. I feel like maybe it was too thick."

"Sophie, your spanakopita looked really good too," Maura added.

I was buoyed by the compliment; I'd noticed we were all stingier with them these days than we had been the first week. "I hope it was fancy enough for them," I said. "I can't tell what they want from me."

Stan rolled his eyes. "Oh, come on, Soph, you know you're gonna win this one."

"No, I don't!" I insisted.

"You made your own phyllo dough."

"Yeah, but I used the pasta maker to do it. My grandfather would call that cheating. And when Patricia asked me if I knew arugula originated from the Mediterranean, I said no."

"I would have lied," Stan said. "But, please, this isn't a history competition; this is a cooking competition."

The truth was, I did feel good about my chances. Better than good. By the time the door cracked open forty-five minutes later and a PA told us the judges were ready, I was confident, maybe too confident.

We trooped back into the kitchen, exhausted and rumpled, and lined up in front of Patricia, Chef Bouchard, Stefan, and virtual Tommy, who was joining us from Belgium.

"Chefs," Tommy began, "this was a very close one, but the judges have reached a decision. Britney." Britney stepped forward. "Your pasta was simple, but the flavors shone. It was a perfect summer pasta. Once again, beautifully plated."

Tommy looked to Patricia. "Shelby," she continued, and Shelby stood at attention. "The crust on your chicken piccata was perfect, and the lemon and capers balanced nicely against your raisin pilaf."

"Thank you, Chef," Shelby said.

My earlier confidence was quickly evaporating. Maybe my spanakopita hadn't been the home run I thought it was.

"And Sophie," Chef Bouchard said. The nervous knot in my stomach loosened. "We were extremely impressed you made your own phyllo, though it could have been a bit thinner. The addition of mint and parsley to the spanakopita filling was also a nice touch. Overall, it was a well thought out and executed dish."

The judges betrayed nothing with their faces.

Tommy finally spoke. "It was a very hard decision this week." Dramatic pause. "But there can only be one chef at the top of the class. And this week's winner is . . ."

I held my breath.

". . . Shelby."

I was shocked, the defeat like a punch to the solar plexus. I had truly believed it was my week.

"Sophie," Patricia said as the other chefs congratulated an equally surprised Shelby, "you were very close."

I wanted to tell Patricia that all the second and third places in the world didn't matter if I couldn't win this one challenge. What had all those years in the Taverna Ristorante kitchen taught me, if not how to ace a Mediterranean cooking test? But the cameras were rolling. I put on a smile and hugged Shelby. "Congratulations," I said.

"Thank you," she whispered in my ear. "And sorry."

A grip was fiddling with a light in the Box. A Kitchen Confidential was the last thing I wanted to be doing after losing the Mediterranean challenge, but the MIB wanted my reaction to Shelby's win. "Are we ready?" he asked the grip impatiently.

"Yes. Sorry," the guy said, giving it one last look and shuffling out of the room.

"Sorry about that," Peter said to me. "We'll get started." The camera was already running behind him.

"No problem."

"Tell me how you feel about the competition today. You lost."

He didn't say "test." He said "competition." He didn't say, "You got second place." He said, "You lost." No sugarcoating there. I wasn't at the top of the class; therefore, I'd failed.

"I'm disappointed. Obviously. I thought I could win this one."

"How do you feel you did? Were you happy with your dish?"

"I thought my spanakopita was a home run. I thought I'd pulled it off. I could have done better, I guess. You can always do better."

"Do you think Shelby should have won?"

"What do you mean?"

The MIB looked a bit annoyed by my question; his had been clear enough. "Do you think Shelby deserved to be at the top of the class this week?"

"I guess." I shrugged. "I didn't try Shelby's dish, so I don't know. I think chicken piccata can be too salty, but the judges liked it. It must have been good."

"What's your relationship with Shelby like?"

"We're friends."

Peter paused to listen to someone speaking in his earpiece. Then, "Sorry," he said, "can you say that again? But use her name, so we know who you're talking about."

This was weird. "Shelby and I are friends."

"Would you say that you're jealous of her?"

"No," I said, starting to get annoyed myself.

"What's she like?"

"She's really talented." In my opinion, Shelby was one of the best chefs on the show. "She'll be famous one day."

"What's Shelby like as a person?"

I was well aware that Shelby had beaten me in the all-important Meditcrranean test, but lhis was ridiculous. The MIB was shooting his questions at me in a rapid-fire succession that barely gave me time to think. "I don't know. I mean she's nice and smart. She's funny. She's super motivated and kind of competitive."

"How does that make you feel?"

"What?"

"When Shelby gets competitive, how does it make you feel?"

My mind went, of course, to the burn book and the fact that it existed at all. "Sometimes it's hard when she gets competitive. But I think she means well. Shelby just really wants to win."

"Do you think she will?"

"I don't know who will win. Honestly. Some people have surprised me."

"Care to elaborate?"

I smiled. "Not really."

"Okay," Peter said. "Good job today, Sophie. Enjoy your weekend."

I thought of Luc's invitation. "I will," I said.

I'd been so weirded out by my Kitchen Confidential with the MIB that I called an emergency meeting of Team S on the patio that night after the mics were off.

Shelby was steaming. "So they wanted you to talk smack about me, basically?" she clarified.

"Basically, yeah. It was like they were trying to start a fight."

"How did I not see this?" Stan cried, his palms smacking his forehead as if all the mystery of the universe had just been revealed to him. "It's so obvious. We've been focusing on the other contestants, but . . . you finding that notebook the week of the Mediterranean challenge . . . the leading questions in your Confidential. My horoscope had said that the beginning of this month would see turmoil when Mercury went retrograde and to be careful of people with ulterior motives entering my sphere."

"Stanley, use standard English, please."

Stan ignored Shelby. "They're baiting you. Sophie, I think the *MIB* wanted *you* to find Shelby's notebook. I think he arranged it."

"It wasn't my notebook anymore," Shelby clarified, something she felt the need to do every time we mentioned it now.

"Of course not, doll. But they wanted Sophie to believe it was. Think about it. When the MIB saw that notebook the first day, he knew it was valuable. It was a potential tool. Reality shows thrive on drama. Who wants to watch a bunch of teenagers cook all day unless there's gonna be name calling and weave pulling?"

"Weave pulling?" I asked dubiously.

"Please, I know you've seen *Charm School*. They were just trying to stir up a little controversy. They want us to turn on each other."

Shelby was chewing on the ends of her hair thoughtfully. "Maybe," she said. "Think about all the strange stuff that's been happening lately. Remember when Mario was convinced someone had moved his salmon from the walk-in? Maybe it wasn't Maura. . . ."

I thought back on the past couple of weeks. At times, things had felt . . . sketchy. Once I'd also thought my tray of tandoori chicken had been moved. I'd found it on another pan rack and just assumed the stress was messing with my memory. But there were definitely less ingredients to go around these days, and I could have sworn the kitchen felt warmer, as if someone had turned down the a.c. It was like they wanted us to argue.

I connected the dots Stan was laying out. "So do you think the MIB wrote that stuff in the burn book?"

Stan considered this for a second. "No," he said decidedly. "I don't think he wrote it. *Fluffball* doesn't strike me as a regular part of his vocabulary. And he can't tell baba ghanoush from béarnaise."

"Then who wrote it?" I asked.

"That I don't know. I still think it was one of the other contestants."

"And how would the MIB know Sophie would find it?" Shelby asked. "It's not like she normally goes through my locker. Do you?" she said suddenly.

"No!"

It seemed a complicated plot to orchestrate. Then again, the MIB's questions in my Kitchen Confidential had felt so pointed. He was definitely fixated on feeding any tension between me and Shelby.

"I feel so used," I said, only half joking.

Shelby had a fire in her eyes I'd only seen before in the kitchen. "We'll get to the bottom of this," she said.

Stan nodded. "Nobody puts Team S in a corner."

Shelby and Stan were going to be cheesy tourists and see California's very own Old Faithful in Calistoga with Philip, Mario, and Britney. Stan agreed to go, he said, only because Shelby insisted the trip was an opportunity to find out what the other chefs knew about the burn book. I thought it had more to do with the fact Philip was going. Shelby wouldn't say much about her investigation, except that her strategy was to "divide and conquer."

As much as I also wanted to know who had written those things in the burn book, my mind was made up. I would be taking a chance meeting Luc by the loading dock—whatever adventure it was he had in mind for us, I had the feeling it didn't involve a cameraman—but if the producers were going to play dirty, so was I. That morning at breakfast, I pulled Stan and Shelby into the women's bathroom and locked the door. I signaled for them to switch off their mics.

"The Frenchie?" Stan asked wide-eyed when I told him about my plan to meet Luc. "Ooh, la la. Where are you going?"

"I don't know."

"Would you consider leaving your mic on, for my sake?" Stan asked with a salacious gleam in his eye.

"Stan!" I slapped at his arm. I was blushing now.

"What *are* you going to do about the mic?" Shelby asked. The producers had started asking us to wear our wireless microphones all the time, even on our down days. Since we weren't technically "working" on the weekends, I wondered if this new rule was fair and even legal.

"I guess I'll have to turn it off," I said. I couldn't be sure of the mic's range, or where Luc was taking me. I was sure, however, that Maura and Britney had gotten a stern warning just last Wednesday for taking their mics off early.

"Bad girl!" Stan exclaimed with a wicked smile.

"Are you really going to turn it off?" Shelby asked.

I felt emboldened by the idea. It made me nervous, of course, to disobey the MIB, but he hadn't exactly earned my loyalty. I didn't like being manipulated. "Yes," I said, resolve replacing any apprehension. "They can't just keep changing the rules. Besides, they want drama; I'll give them drama."

"You know that could get you in big trouble," Shelby said.

"Only if they catch me." Who was I?

"Okay," she sighed. "Good luck!"

Spanakopita (Spinach Pie)

I could eat this Greek spinach pie every day. Pappou would say using store-bought phyllo is blasphemous, but unless you're trying to impress a panel of celebrity chefs, I'd recommend it. You can find it in the freezer section. You can also use frozen spinach. Either way, just make sure to drain it, or you'll have spinach soup. Nutmeg adds a touch of sweet spice to the filling, and the mint and parsley up the freshness factor. Be careful not to tear the phyllo sheets. They're more temperamental than Raffi in the mornings.

SERVES 4 to 6

Ingredients

2 pounds fresh baby spinach (or substitute frozen)
3 tablespoons olive oil
2 leeks, white and light green parts, well rinsed and thinly sliced
3 cloves garlic, minced
2 cups crumbled feta cheese
1/2 cup finely chopped fresh mint
1/2 cup finely chopped parsley
1 teaspoon ground nutmeg (freshly grated is best)
1 teaspoon freshly ground black pepper
2 large eggs, lightly beaten
10 frozen phyllo pastry sheets, thawed
8 tablespoons unsalted butter, melted

Directions

1. Preheat oven to 350° F. Lightly grease a 9″×11″ or 9″×13″ baking dish with butter.

2. Heat oil in an extra-large skillet over medium heat. Add leeks and garlic; cook, stirring occasionaly, until soft and fragrant, about 4 minutes. Add spinach in handfuls, letting it wilt before folding in more. When all spinach is cooked down, remove from heat and transfer to a colander over the sink. Gently press out any excess liquid. Set aside to cool. Once cool, add feta, mint, parsley, pepper, nutmeg, and eggs. Combine well.

3. Place 1 phyllo rectangle on the counter. (Cover the rest with plastic wrap and a damp cloth to keep it from drying out while you work.) With a pastry or basting brush, gently brush or dab the phyllo sheet with melted butter. Carefully place a second sheet on top of the first; brush it with butter. Repeat until you have a stack of 5 sheets of phyllo. Repeat whole process for a second stack of 5 sheets.

4. Line the bottom of your baking dish with 1 stack of phyllo, pressing into the corners. Trim excess with a paring knife. Spread spinach filling evenly over the phyllo. Cover with the second stack of phyllo, trimming around the edges of the dish. Brush the top generously

with butter. Using a sharp knife, score the top layer of phyllo to allow steam to escape while baking.

5. Bake for 35 to 40 minutes, or until the phyllo is golden brown. Remove from oven and let rest for about 10 minutes. Cut into squares and serve warm or at room temperature.

Chapter Eleven

I felt like Jason Bourne as I snuck around the corner of the main building to the decidedly less picturesque loading docks. Because it was Saturday, the ramps were empty and the doors were rolled down. A few cardboard boxes and wooden crates littered the area, but other than a stray cat prowling for mice, I didn't see any movement.

I looked around. "Hello?" I said. My mic was still on—for now. I didn't want to cut through the clutter of the microphone chatter the PAs were probably monitoring with anything too exciting.

The low rumble of an engine grew louder, and Luc appeared around the other side of the building, looking very French on a white Vespa scooter. He stopped in front of me. "You came," he said.

"I shouldn't have."

"Do you always do what you should?" It sounded like a challenge.

I put a finger to my lips, not wanting him to say anything more until I reached around and flipped the switch on my microphone. It was done.

Luc raised an eyebrow. "I guess not!"

He handed me a helmet, which I strapped under my chin, tucking my ponytail up into it. I put on some sunglasses. Incognito. "I've never been on one of these," I said, climbing onto the back of the scooter.

Luc laughed. "Ah, Sophie, there's a first time for everything," he said, and we were off.

I closed my eyes and held on to his waist. Soon we were a few miles from the NCA. My hair had fallen out of my helmet and was whipping around my face as we sped down a side road. I wasn't afraid of the Vespa but didn't mind the excuse to snuggle up to Luc's back. He smelled like cinnamon and soap. The warmth of his body and the sun on my face after a long week under television lights was heavenly.

Luc still hadn't told me where we were going, only that he wanted to show me one of his favorite places in the valley. We turned down a narrow lane. As we drove farther, the neatly contoured vineyards that flanked the road, with their evenly spaced rows of grapevines lashed to metal and cable supports, suddenly gave way to a wilder patch of land. Here the vines were gnarled and overgrown, crowded by blackberry brambles and weeds. The lines in which they were planted were less visible.

Luc pulled the Vespa over to the side of the road, and we climbed off. "What is this?" I asked.

He grabbed a basket from the back of the bike, an old wicker picnic basket. It was so classic and cute, and yet he was so unaware that some boys—boys like Alex, it crossed my mind—might not be caught dead riding around on a white scooter with vintage picnic baskets.

"It was a vineyard, a good one once, my father says, but they went out of business a few years ago." He stepped between the rusted wires of an old fence, holding it open for me as I did the same. "This is how much work it takes to keep a vineyard producing. Only three years, and it's already overgrown." He handled a leaf on one of the withered vines.

"Wow," I said. "So it's abandoned?"

"Someone still owns it, but they're not getting wine out of it any time soon—at least not good wine!" He smiled.

Luc walked a few yards into the field. I followed. He stopped in a clear space between what was once two neat, staked rows of grapevines. He opened a flap on the picnic basket and pulled out two giant beach towels and laid them on the ground next to each other to form a picnic blanket.

"Please forgive me for the towels," he said apologetically. "They were all I could find at my father's."

"I think I can find it in my heart," I said, sitting on the larger, striped towel.

He looked at me questioningly. "No problem," I translated, realizing the expression was a foreign one to him. "So we're having a picnic?"

Luc sat beside me. He pulled the basket over and started laying its contents on the towel between us. "Yes."

"Good. I like picnics."

"Good. I like that you like picnics."

I made a face. "Are you making fun of me?"

"Of course not!" Now he made a face, teasing me.

Luc set out green and black olives, several hunks of cheese, dried apricots, pistachios, a salami, and a baguette on our makeshift picnic blanket. It was a feast, and still more was coming from the basket. "I hope you like my choices," he said.

"I do! It's like Californian antipasto," I said, referring to the selection of appetizers Italians serve before a meal.

He took the lid off the container of glistening olives and held it out to me. I plucked one and popped it in my mouth. "I love olives."

"These are grown one valley over."

It was delicious—meaty and salty, and I had no idea what to do with the pit. Luc wrestled with the wrapping on a salami, and I surreptitiously spit it into my hand and dumped it over my shoulder into the brush.

Luc took a knife from the basket and sliced the salami. He speared a piece and handed it to me on the point of the knife. "This is the best salami in Napa," he said, cutting a piece for himself.

"Oh, my gosh." The salami was amazing—complex and slightly spicy. "Oh, my gosh!"

Luc laughed. "Do you like drunken goat cheese?"

"Drunken goat cheese? Do the goats that make it have an alcohol problem?"

He laughed again. I was doing well, I thought. Keep it up.

"They are party animals." If Alex had made that joke I would have had made fun of him, but I figured it was all right for an exchange student—or for Luc. "It is goat cheese soaked in red wine for two or three days, which gives the rind its purple color." He ran his finger along the burgundy edge of the otherwise off-white cheese. "Here. Try some."

He carved a sliver. Like the time our toes touched in the grape-stomping vat at Clos d'Été, I was hyperaware that our fingers brushed as he handed it to me, and I wondered if he'd meant to touch me.

A girl could get used to this. A private picnic in the middle of a Napa vineyard with a delectable French hottie hand-feeding me equally delectable morsels of food. . . . When was I waking up from this dream? Not soon, I hoped.

"It's delicious," I said. "Pretty mild for a goat cheese."

Luc nodded eagerly. "If you try, you can actually taste what the goats ate."

I lifted a suspicious eyebrow. "Seriously?"

"Yes, seriously! Smell it." He held the cheese to my face. I inhaled. It smelled like cheese to me, but Luc continued. "Eating is not just about tasting. It is about experiencing the food. You see it, you smell it, you taste it, you touch it, you feel it."

"Do you hear it?" I asked.

He considered this for a moment. "If it is crunchy, you might hear it."

"I meant, does your food talk to you?"

He laughed and held an olive to his ear. He nodded his

head as if it was telling him a secret. "Aha. Yes. Very interesting." He popped the olive in his mouth. "He had a death wish."

It was my turn to laugh. "Wow, the way you talk about food . . . I don't know that I've ever . . . I don't know, experienced it like that."

"You haven't?" Luc asked, surprised.

I shook my head, and the silence around us suddenly overwhelmed me. No production crew, no cameras, no booms or cables or lights—just the quiet of the valley and the sunshine. And Luc.

"I have an idea," he said.

Leaning back on my elbows, I hoped I looked casual instead of as awkward and nervous as I felt. I squinted up at him. The sun was behind him, so all I could see was a corona of light behind Luc's head. "What's that?" I asked.

"Do you trust me?" he said, for the second time, I realized, in two days.

I cocked my head and screwed my mouth to the side like I was considering the question. Luc jogged back to the Vespa, where he produced a navy blue cotton scarf from a compartment under the seat. Only a French guy, I thought again.

He had decided I should explore the rest of the picnic basket blindfolded, to better savor the flavors. "Like how blind people's other senses are heightened?" I asked.

"*Exactement*," he answered. He tied the scarf around my eyes, and the shadow of his hand passed in front of my face as he checked that I couldn't see. Then he proceeded to feed me.

"What do you taste?" he asked.

"I don't know," I said.

"Think about it. What do you taste?"

I let everything else around me fade away as I focused on the tastes on my tongue. This was another cheese, a local one, he said. "It's earthy . . . and subtle," I answered. "I feel like I can almost taste . . . grass."

"Yes! Exactly."

I smiled at my correct answer, and the weight of Luc's hand suddenly resting on my knee let loose a flutter in my chest.

"Now try this," he said, and his fingers touched my lips as they slipped something sweet in between them, a piece of nectarine. Playfully I pretended to bite at his finger.

"Hey!"

"It tastes . . . French."

He laughed. "Is that a good thing?"

I couldn't see anything beneath my blindfold, but I could feel him leaning closer. His face was only inches from mine.

"A very good thing."

I waited for him to kiss me, my eyes closed under the blindfold and my lips slightly parted, just as I'd been taught by every movie I'd ever seen. But it didn't happen. I waited another moment, and still no kiss.

Self-consciously, I pulled the edge of the blindfold up so I could see. Luc was stretching his neck and listening. I looked in the direction where his eyes searched, and then I saw and heard it also: a van was turning from the main highway onto the road—a white van that looked an awful lot like the vans the *TTK* crew used.

Luc snorted in disbelief. "Your show has found us, I think."

"How?" I asked, sounding far more panicked than he did. "Do they have a homing device?" Couldn't they give me privacy for just two hours?

"Maybe they do?"

"I wouldn't put it past them. Where can we go?" My adrenaline was pumping.

"I don't know," Luc said, "but we'll figure it out."

He started throwing the leftover food and utensils into the basket. I balled up the two towels and stuffed them in on top of the food. We sprinted to the Vespa and hopped on. I glanced back at the van. I couldn't make out the faces of the driver and passenger at this distance and hoped they couldn't make out mine.

Luc started to do a U-turn that would send us past the van to get back to the main road. "Wait!" I shouted into his ear, under his helmet. "They'll see me. Can we go the other way?"

"It's a dead end. It just leads to the old winery. We could hide there?" Luc turned his U-turn into a circle, heading down the road away from the van again.

"No," I said, realizing this was ridiculous. I'd done the crime; I'd have to do the time. "You can turn around," I said, wondering if the producers would snatch me into the open doors of the moving van like a kidnapping victim. Would Luc get in trouble?

He turned the Vespa around yet again. It must have looked to whoever was in the van like we were doing doughnuts. "Do you want to talk to them?" Luc asked.

"I guess I should," I answered, defeated—and terrified.

Luc slowed and put his foot down to steady us as we came to a halt. I climbed off the scooter, removing my helmet. The van didn't stop. It didn't even slow down. As it passed us, the driver waved. I thought I might see the MIB in the passenger seat, but I didn't recognize either of the men. To my relieved astonishment, the words stenciled on the side of the van read VALLEY ELECTRIC: OUR CUSTOMERS COME FIRST.

As the van trundled down the road toward the winery, I exhaled. I turned to Luc, laughing like a crazy person. "That wasn't them. That wasn't them!"

He smiled, laughing not at that fact but at me. "A narrow escape," he agreed.

With our picnic cut short, Luc wondered if there was anything else in the valley I wanted to see. I thought about it. "There's something I want *you* to see," I said.

When we got to the Last Supper, the kitchen was already hitting its stride for dinner prep. A menu board displayed the dishes for the evening, and chefs were chopping, dicing, mixing, boiling, and reducing away.

"Sophie!" Aunt Mary said, surprised to see me. She wiped her hands on her apron as she came out from behind the line to hug me. "This is an unexpected surprise." Then she noticed Luc. "Good to see you, Luc." The huge smile she gave me as she said it made me blush.

"I know you're busy," I said quickly. "But I kind of pulled a jailbreak. I wanted Luc to see your kitchen. Do you think maybe we could hide out here for a little while?"

"Of course! If you're willing to work."

Luc clapped his hands together and smiled at me. "Always!"

In the corner of the kitchen, out of the way of the regular hustle and bustle, Luc and I shelled edamame for a salad with mint, feta, and almonds and talked about what dishes I'd cook if I made it to the finale. It was the first time I'd allowed myself to imagine getting there. I was flip-flopping between a lobster ravioli or something with lamb. Luc wouldn't tell me his opinion. "It has to come from your heart," he said.

"How's it going?" Aunt Mary asked, coming over and running her hands through the edamame-feta-mint mixture. "Ah!" she said, deeply inhaling the smell of the fresh mint. "*C'est magnifique*. Luc, you can work for me anytime."

"Hey!" I said.

My aunt squeezed her arm around my shoulders. "Of course my niece has a job here anytime she wants it as well."

"So you are Sophie's aunt?" Luc said.

I nodded. "My mother's sister."

"Gosh," Aunt Mary said, looking at me intently, as if suddenly gripped by a very strong emotion. "It's been years, though, hasn't it? I'm sorry, Sophie. I should have visited. It was just so hard. And then it had been so long."

I shrugged. "You sent postcards and presents."

She moved beside me at the counter so that the three of us were working side by side. "I still remember when your mom met your father," she said.

"Really?" This I hadn't heard before. Of course I knew the basics from my father—that my mother was the most beautiful woman he had ever met, that it was love at first sight, all the stuff kids usually hear, especially ones who've lost a parent—but never the whole story. For a Greek-Italian, my father was a miserable storyteller. He got distracted too easily. He'd start with a story about my mother and end up talking about the time he ran with the bulls in Pamplona.

"Oh, yeah," Mary said. Her hands worked much quicker than mine or Luc's as she shelled. "Like it was yesterday. Your mom and I were backpacking through Europe. We'd found this tiny little taverna literally clinging to the cliff-side in Thíra. I don't even think it had a name. The waiter was young, just a little older than us, and cute—your mom thought so more than I did. She had just broken up with her boyfriend back home, and this trip was sort of a forget-what's-his-face adventure."

Luc and I both laughed. I wondered if he had a what's-her-face back in Paris.

"Turns out he was the son of the owners, a Greek man and an Italian woman, and eventually . . . your father! He took us around the island and to the volcano—which I thought smelled like rotten eggs, but which totally worked on your mother—and that was that. I was meeting some friends in Palermo, so I left the next day, but your mother stayed."

Aunt Mary laughed and looked off into the distance, as if she was seeing it all happen again. "Your grandparents were furious with me for leaving her. And even more furious when she came home engaged!"

"They barely knew each other!" I said.

"Yep. They'd been dating two months. They kept writing

letters for another six months, and then he moved to the U.S. to marry her."

"Wow," Luc said, crumbling some feta. "He must have really loved her."

"He did," I said quietly.

"And he had to walk through fire to prove it!" Aunt Mary added. "Mom and Dad always thought Susannah would marry a banker or lawyer, one of Dad's golf buddies' sons. And here came this cocky Mediterranean charmer sweeping their daughter off her feet." She laughed.

"They were about as different as night and day, outwardly at least. But they loved each other, and Mom and Dad eventually came around, once they saw it. That restaurant was as much your mother's dream as your father's. She was a teacher, but she wanted to be a chef."

"I have all her old cookbooks," I said.

This made my aunt smile. "You do?"

"Yeah."

"We'd talked about opening a restaurant together before your dad came along. That's what inspired me to come out here and open this place." Aunt Mary looked around and smiled wistfully. "The name was Susannah's idea. She always said you should eat every meal as if it were your last. You remind me a lot of her, Sophie."

This surprised me. I often looked for myself in my father or my grandparents, finding my thick, brown hair and substantial hips or my quick-to-anger, quick-to-forget temperament. Maybe I forgot to look for my mother, not really sure what I'd be looking for.

Aunt Mary's story made me both happy and sad, one of

those messy emotions that twists your insides but leaves you wanting to hear more. Why did I have to come to California to hear that story? I knew my father resented my aunt for leaving us to come to Napa, but she was following her dreams, and it seemed she'd kept my mother's memory alive more than anyone.

I wanted more stories. But the more I knew my mother, or knew the woman she had been—the kind of woman who fell in love with dashing foreign men she hardly knew, who backpacked around Europe and taught herself to cook—the sharper her absence was. Before I came face-to-face with my aunt again, my mother had been neatly contained in the stack of cookbooks piled by my bed. I got a whiff of her in the smell of baking bread or a taste in a recipe she had dog-eared, but she was no more real to me than Julia Child or James Beard, or Tommy Chang, for that matter. Until now.

As Luc and I left the restaurant later that afternoon, I felt the pressure behind my eyes begin to build. I didn't want to cry, not in front of him. I barely ever cried about my mother. How could I, when I'd never known her?

But Luc must have noticed that I was unusually quiet or heard a sniffle as I tried to push back the tears. We stopped at the Vespa. "Are you okay, Sophie?" he asked, not sounding terribly surprised to see me upset. I thought I'd been better at covering it.

I bit my lip and a tear, against my will, slid down my cheek. My gaze fixed on the gravel parking lot. Without saying anything more, Luc gently lifted my chin so that our eyes met. He wiped away another tear and then another, and I thought he would kiss me this time, but again, he didn't. He pulled me into a hug. It was perfect. Too perfect. And if I knew anything, it was that perfect never lasted. I didn't trust perfect.

After a minute of burying my face in Luc's shirt, I climbed onto the Vespa, and we drove back to the NCA. It was still early, and I hoped I could slip into the dorm without anyone noticing. The silence on my mic, however, I would have a hard time explaining. I would deal with it, I decided, when the time came.

"There you are." Shelby yanked me into our room, quickly shutting the door behind me. She opened it again to do a left-right glance down the hall. "Phew," she puffed, closing the door again.

I braced for impact. "I'm in trouble, aren't I?"

"Is it still off?" she mouthed, pointing at the mic pack clipped to my jeans.

"Yeah. Is yours?" I pointed at the mic clipped to her shorts.

"I just flipped it off when I saw you," she answered in a normal voice. "And no, you're not in trouble—thanks to me. You're sick. If anyone asks how you're feeling, you're better."

"Okay."

"One of the production assistants noticed you weren't with us at Old Faithful—really stupid sight, by the way: a slimy, stinky pond that shot water every thirty minutes. Oh, and there were fainting goats."

"Fainting goats?"

"And llamas. Not important." Shelby was talking so

fast, I could barely keep up with her. "The important thing is that a PA asked why you hadn't come with us. I said you weren't feeling well. Then later I heard that PA and another PA talking about how they hadn't heard from your mic all day. So I told them you had explosive diarrhea."

"What! On camera? You told America that I had explosive diarrhea?"

"I don't remember if they were taping at that point or not. Like I said, the place was kind of boring. Don't worry. I'm sure they'd edit it out anyway. And you should be thanking me! They were getting suspicious that your mic was silent, so I told them you turned it off—you know, because of the ED. I told them it might be food poisoning. That got them freaking out."

"Crap."

"Seriously." Shelby giggled.

"Shelby. Did they send someone to check on me?"

"Sorry. I'm not sure. If they did, just tell them you found a bathroom in another building so you could have more privacy."

I paced the room, breathing deeply as the information set in. "Okay. Do you think I should turn my mic back on?"

"Yes, and I should too."

"Shelby, wait—before you do . . . thank you." If there had been any lingering doubt in my mind over her intentions and the notebook, it was gone now. I could trust Shelby. Which reminded me: "Did you find out anything about the burn book?"

She screwed up her eyebrows. "Not yet, but I think I've got a suspect."

"Who?"

"I'll tell you tonight when we're off mic again. You might want to skip dinner, by the way. I'll bring you some crackers or something. That'll look good."

I'd eaten so much with Luc at the restaurant that that wouldn't be a problem. I reached around and flipped the switch on my microphone. Shelby did the same.

"Hey, Sophie," she said in a stage voice I hoped didn't sound too unnatural to anyone listening in, "are you feeling better?"

"Yeah." I moaned slightly. "It must have been something I ate. I found a bathroom in the main building."

"You didn't want to stink up the dorm? You know, with your explosive diarrhea?" Shelby said extra loud. She was enjoying this.

My jaw dropped. "Yeah," I said, desperately trying not to laugh out loud as I chased Shelby around the room, swatting at her. "Because of that."

She dove for her bed to escape my reach. "Because of your explosive diarrhea?"

"Yes. And the vomiting."

"Gross. Well, I'm glad you're feeling better."

"Me too."

Five minutes later, Megan the assistant producer was at our door. Someone had heard our conversation. I was lying in bed in sweatpants and a T-shirt, my hair mussed. Shelby had flicked water on my face to look like I'd been sweating. While obviously ticked at my afternoon of silence, Megan didn't argue much with my excuse of embarrassing bodily functions. I supposed she wouldn't want her bathroom life monitored by a television crew either, or else the producers were scared they'd given a kid food poisoning. She left our room with a few words of both concern and caution: If I didn't start to feel better, they would get a doctor. And my mic should not go off again.

Week 5

LATIN CUISINE

Chapter Twelve

Adobo, sofrito, *pimentón*, yuca, cacao—I thought I knew Spanish from working in Taverna Ristorante's kitchen, but my vocabulary had grown exponentially that week. A guest chef from the NCA faculty was teaching our Latin course. But while we were learning mole sauce and empanadas, Shelby, Stan, and I had become more focused on the mystery of the burn book. Stan liked to come up with ridiculous conspiracy theories that involved the U.S. government and Scientology, but Shelby, who seemed to feel especially violated, as it had been her notebook, was really obsessed.

Her first suspicions, she told us after their trip to Old Faithful, had revolved around Philip. When Stan heard this and started to object, however, Shelby silenced him. She had quickly discarded that theory, she said, for another one. The culprit was Dante, for two reasons: (1) Shelby remembered seeing him speaking privately with a producer a few days before I found the book. This was not strange in and of itself, except that Shelby saw the producer switch off Dante's mic while they talked. And (2) Dante had been the one to spill the tomato sauce on my uniform, which sent me to Shelby's locker in the first place. There were a number of holes in Shelby's theory, the first of which was how the producers would know she would offer her clean jacket to me. "What? Was Stan gonna offer his?" Shelby asked. "Trust me. Dante wrote that stuff in the notebook. It's always the quiet ones."

The three of us met in our pajamas late one night in our dorm room. We weren't supposed to have members of the opposite sex in our rooms, but we figured no one would accuse Stan of getting frisky, with us at least.

Shelby was grilling me for the details leading up to my finding the burn book in her locker. "Did you tell anyone that you were wearing your spare uniform that day?" she asked.

I thought back. "No. But I'd mentioned to a PA that I needed my laundry done."

"Well, whoever planted the 'new and improved' notebook in my locker knew that I had a clean uniform in there and knew that I would offer it to you. All Dante had to do was dirty up the one you were wearing."

"It still seems like a stretch," I said, ever the hopeful—or naive—skeptic. "A lot could go wrong with that plan."

"They had nothing to lose if it did go wrong," said Shelby. "And it didn't. The producers' goal was to create drama, and it worked." Shelby was pacing the room while Stan and I watched her from my bottom bunk. She was on a roll. "But they needed help from the inside. And Dante's the most logical conclusion. He's the only one, other than me—cleared of all charges—who had any direct action leading to your finding of the burn book. He spilled the sauce."

"I don't know if I'd call it a 'logical' conclusion," I said.

"What if it was a group job?" Stan asked, egging Shelby on. "What if everyone's in on it except for us? How do we even know you're really innocent?"

Shelby narrowed her eyes. "Don't be stupid, Stan. Okay, I've got a plan. Dante and Mario are like BFFs, right?"

"They're no Team S," Stan said with a cocky wag of his head.

"This is true," Shelby allowed. "They're no Team S. But they are friends, and I'll bet if Dante had the notebook, he showed it to Mario or told him about it. Now, Dante's a smart one. If I approached him, he'd deny it all. But if I had information from Mario . . ."

"Is this giving you chills?" Stan asked, pushing up the sleeve of his shirt to show goose bumps. "Because this is giving me chills."

"Listen to me, Stanley," Shelby said. "If I go to Dante with some leverage, we may just get him to sing like a canary. Mario is the weaker link. We start there."

"Bravo," Stan said, clapping. "This is better than *Law & Order*."

"Oh, yeah," Shelby said. An audience was all she needed to get worked up. "Play with fire, Dante, and you'll get burned."

Finally we were allowed to write back to our families. The producers had given us each a postcard of Napa and fifteen minutes. *Dear Dad, Raffi, Nonna, and Pappou . . .* My pen hesitated for a moment as I wondered whether to include Alex. It wasn't as if I was dating Alex. I had decided his signature under the words *love* and *miss* on my family's postcard meant something only in my warped brain. Still, lately, when I thought about Luc and the day we spent together, I felt almost guilty, like I was cheating. But if it was cheating, I realized, then it was cheating in a one-way relationship.

And Alex, I wrote. *Greetings from California!* We weren't allowed to write anything about the show itself, and I knew the producers would be reading them, so I kept it short and sweet: *The past four and a half weeks have been amazing. I've learned so much and have met some really great people. I'm tired!* I wondered if the sleep deprivation was all right to talk about. *But it's worth it. Even if I miss you.* Like Crazystan, I wanted to write. *Wish you were here. Mean it.*

I signed it quickly, before I could overthink it. *Love, Sophie.*

"*No está trabajando,*" Shelby said on Friday.

"What's not working?" I asked as I dusted my chiles rellenos in flour and then dipped them in batter. The ones I'd made in lab earlier that week had come out a little dry but pretty tasty. "Why are you speaking Spanish?"

She pointed at her mic. "*Mario no está hablando,*" she whispered from the side of her mouth. Mario's not talking.

I had almost forgotten Shelby's new plan to "isolate and interrogate." It seemed her plans often consisted of two intimidating verbs. Still, that did not explain why she was now speaking to me in Spanish.

"Hmm," I mused distractedly, wanting to focus more on my dish than on unraveling the secret of the mysterious burn book. "Have you already finished your enchiladas?"

"My tomatillos are roasting," she answered, glancing across the kitchen suspiciously at the MIB. "In Spanish," she whispered almost inaudibly. "So *they* don't hear." She pointed again at her mic.

The kitchen was hot, the food was hot, and I was hot. All I wanted at the moment was to turn out the best chiles rellenos I could. "Maybe *they* speak Spanish too," I whispered, pointing at my own mic. This ticked her off. "Can we talk about this later?" I asked. I still had to fry my chiles and plate them before we presented our dishes to the judges.

"Fine," she huffed.

"*Gracias,*" I said, trying not to laugh.

I was definitely not laughing two hours later when Mario and his smoked chili-rubbed brisket won the challenge. Perhaps I shouldn't have been surprised that the Hispanic kid won the Latin test, but it did make my loss the previous week sting a little more. It also did nothing for Mario's case with Shelby.

"The price of silence?" Shelby said. She nodded at Mario bragging to Britney about the set of Le Creuset cookware he'd won.

I, for one, was too exhausted for conspiracy theories. Perhaps karma had caught up with me as well, because now my stomach really was doing somersaults. I blamed the spicy food and told Shelby I'd meet her back at our room after her Kitchen Confidential.

My desk was usually cluttered with dirty clothes and

makeup, unlike Shelby's, which was neat and clean, with everything at right angles. But when I walked through the door, something on top of my mess immediately caught my attention. There was a huge bouquet of pink roses.

My first response was to look for the cameraman swooping in for my reaction, but the only person in my doorway was Stan. "*Hola* . . . ," he started. Then noticing the flowers, "Who are those from?" He rushed to read the card.

"Hey, they're my flowers!" I grabbed the card from his hot little hands.

"Do you think they're from Luc?" he asked, nearly salivating.

For a second, I almost believed they might be. I hadn't noticed the teddy bear in a chef's jacket and toque propped on Shelby's bed. And Stan hadn't found his surprise yet—a massive gift basket from Dean & Deluca.

I read the card out loud. "Good luck with your last two weeks. We're pulling for you! Love, Dad, Raffi, Nonna and Pappou, and Alex."

The producers had let each chef's family send a little pick-me-up to rally us for the last push before finalists were selected. I crumpled on my bed.

"What's wrong?" Stan asked, alarmed. He sat next to me.

The flowers had had the opposite of their intended effect. It was great to hear from my family, of course, but . . . love. Alex. Again. I was confused and lonely and torn. And I had just lost yet another challenge. All I wanted, desperately, was to make them all proud.

"It's just . . . what am I doing here, Stan?" I told myself I wouldn't cry. Anymore.

"What do you mean, 'what are you doing here'?" Stan was almost indignant. "You're cooking your big, fat Greek butt off—I can say that only because I love you and because mine's bigger—and you are knocking 'em dead. You got third place today!"

"Yeah. Third place. I still haven't been at the 'top of the class,' Stan." I mocked the ridiculous lingo of the show. "Not even the week I was supposed to win."

"Neither have I. And you've come in a close second. Plus, I think the Dragon Lady's really taken a liking to you."

It was true that Patricia seemed to have warmed to me since our field trip to the farmers' market. Her exasperation these days was mostly aimed at Maura and, unfortunately, Stan.

"I guess," I said.

"No. No 'I guess.' No pouting. There's no crying in *Teen Test Kitchen*—well, there is, but we'll leave that to Maura. You are a chef, Sophie Nicolaides. So act like one." Stan stood up, his hands clenched in emphatic fists at his sides. "Now I'd better be going before they find me in here and kick us both off for unladylike conduct. We wouldn't want to make Luc jealous, either."

I laughed and threw a balled-up sock at him as he stuck his tongue out and left.

Week 6

PASTRY

Chapter Thirteen

Baking is a very different skill than cooking. It requires precision and the ability to follow directions. Baking is for the obsessive-compulsive. Baking is for people like Shelby. She and Maura were the only cheftestants excited to learn that our last lesson before we competed for spots on the finale was pastry.

There are actually people who weigh their ingredients, because one person's half cup might be different from another person's. Do you scoop, for example, or pour your flour? Believe it or not, this can make a difference. It all seemed like a lot of trouble to me, who was used to measuring things in splashes, dashes, and pinches. The most I'd ever baked was pizza crusts and phyllo—hardly a chocolate genoise (cake) covered in ganache (icing).

Luckily I wasn't the only one who found baking completely foreign.

"Can I substitute baking soda for baking powder?" Britney asked in our first lab.

Philip and Shelby looked at her, horrified. "No!" they said in unison. It was the first time they'd agreed on anything.

On our third afternoon, my coconut cake turned out perfect. It was spongy and light, just like Chef Anne's, the NCA pastry instructor who was teaching us and who insisted we call her by her first name, which made me think of Dr. Phil. My frosting was another story. What should have been smooth and creamy was gloppy and crunchy.

Chef Anne dipped a spoon into the icing bowl. She tasted it. "You forgot the cream of tartar. The sugars crystallized."

I deflated like half the class's pineapple soufflés the day before. "Is it too late to add it now?"

"Yep. Start over."

It felt more like chemistry class than cooking, and there was a reason I'd regularly gotten a C in science. The only real competitors in the test that week were Shelby and Maura, with pecan cream profiteroles and a milk chocolate soufflé, respectively. For the rest of us, our dishes were a joke. I'd copped out with an apple galette that seemed to confirm all the negative assessments of whoever had written in Shelby's notebook. Mario made flan. Philip tried a chile-spiced brownie. Britney made petits fours, which were beautiful but almost inedibly dry. Stan made a heroic attempt at a tiered cinnamon cake with a rolled fondant icing that came out gray and tore when he draped it over the cake. Like me, Dante had gone the fruit route with a simple blackberry cobbler. I wouldn't say that none of us tried, but we might as well have stepped back and let Shelby and Maura take the floor at judges' table.

They called us from the Pressure Cooker after almost an hour of deliberating, during which time we'd wondered if the judges were planning on punishing us by making us eat our own dishes. Plates smeared with Shelby's pecan cream and spoons licked clean of Maura's soufflé were still littering the table in front of the judges. Patricia, however, did not look pleased.

We lined up and waited for the knife to fall. More than for myself, though, I was nervous for Shelby. Beneath her cocky exterior, I knew she just desperately wanted to prove herself, to prove that she was someone bigger and headed for something bigger than what they saw at home in Benton, Wisconsin. How could I not understand that when I felt it so sharply myself? I knew Shelby was destined to be a great chef. She just didn't know it yet, not down in her bones. So I hoped—nothing against Maura—that Shelby would win.

Stefan spoke first. "Chefs, thank you for your desserts today. Some of you were more successful than others." An uneasy chuckle at the understatement passed through everyone but Shelby and Maura. "But there can only be one chef at the top of the class."

Behind Stefan, on the retractable screen, Tommy was beamed in from the set of another TV show—a cooking show or a talk show, I couldn't tell. Like a mirror reflecting a mirror, it was enough to make my mind feel like it might implode.

"Maura," Tommy said, "your soufflé was impeccably

executed and apparently delicious." He nodded at the empty plates in front of the other judges. "Shelby, your profiteroles were airy and light and the pecan cream was silky. I wish I could have tasted both of these."

Tommy paused for effect.

"But the winner this week, taking home a brand-new food processor, courtesy of Cuisinart, is . . . Shelby."

That night the toqued teddy bear sent by her parents was christened Lucky. Shelby, Stan, even Philip, and I toasted her win with sparkling grape juice from Stan's gift basket. In just a week, five of us would be going home for good. Only three would return to film the finale in November. It didn't seem fair that the finalists would be picked based only on our performance in the last test. One bad dish, and six weeks of work would be down the drain. Then again, it was nice to know that the underdogs, like Stan, who had yet to win a week, and me, also had a fighting chance. I'd once been sure Shelby and Philip were a lock for the final three. Sipping my sparkling California grape juice, I decided all bets were off. The finale was any chef's prize to claim.

"You promised him your Cuisinart?" Stan gasped at the sacrilege. "That thing is like the Rolls-Royce of food processors!"

Shelby was telling us how she'd just cornered Mario in the mic-free zone of the boy's bathroom to ask him what he knew about the burn book. When he still wouldn't talk, she'd resorted to bribery. "I also told him that I knew something about Britney he might be interested in hearing."

"What do you know about Britney?" I asked, intrigued myself. Had Shelby, during her preshow research, dug up some deep, dark secret about Britney that she'd managed to keep from us until now?

"That she has a thing for guys with tattoos," Shelby said.

Stan snorted. "How does that help Mario out?"

"I guess it doesn't," said Shelby, "but he got a twenty-cup, eight-hundred-dollar Cuisinart out of the deal!"

"So what did he tell you in exchange?" Stan asked. We had only two minutes left in our bathroom break before we had to report back to the Test Kitchen for our media training seminar that was supposed to prepare us for life in the spotlight once the show aired. The training could have been summed up in four words: Keep your mouth shut. Instead, it was dragging on for hours.

Shelby smirked. She leaned in closer to whisper. "Mario told me that Dante told him that a producer put him up to something that would—quote—'spice things up a bit.'"

"That's it?" I asked.

"What do you mean, 'that's it?'—that's huge! That's confirmation that the MIB is involved in this. They're manipulating us! Who knows what else they've twisted in the name of television!"

"Did he say Dante had written the stuff in the burn book?" Stan asked.

"No," Shelby allowed. "He didn't seem to know about the notebook until I told him, just that Dante was up to something. He said I'd have to ask Dante for more information. But now that I have proof Dante was involved, it's just a matter of the right pressure applied at the right time."

"I hope we're not talking waterboarding," Stan said. Shelby was getting rather intense about this "investigation."

"I'll do it in the walk-in," Shelby said.

"The walk-in fridge?" I clarified. "They don't like us to talk in there."

"Yep," Shelby said with a self-satisfied smile, "because they can't hear us over the mics."

The three minutes that Dante spent with Shelby in the walk-in refrigerator the next day must have been some of the most harrowing of his life, because he finally confessed that a producer had asked him to spill marinara on me—the producer said only to create more drama in the kitchen. Dante maintained, however, that he knew nothing about a notebook in Shelby's locker, let alone that his stunt would lead me to find it. We still didn't know who had written the nasty comments in the burn book, but we were now positive that the producers were behind it.

And Shelby had decided that Tommy Chang needed to know what was really going down on his show. Surely he would be outraged at the unsavory tactics the MIB was employing in his absence. But the only way to get to Tommy without going through the producers was Stefan.

Our final test, which would determine who returned for the finale, was coming up. It was the culmination of all we'd learned over the last six weeks. Our only instruction: to show them what we had. Instead of our usual morning classes and afternoon labs, we had been given four days to test recipes and prep for what, for most of us, would be our final competition on *Teen Test Kitchen*.

One afternoon, Shelby approached Stefan, who was wandering the kitchen answering questions and doling out insults veiled as advice. She said she had something to tell him, but she'd like to speak in private. Stefan's eye twitched, but he agreed and directed her to the locker room. A fitting place, Shelby figured, as this was where the drama had begun. A cameraman tried to follow them, but Stefan waved him off.

The conversation, which Shelby relayed to us later that night, went something like this:

> *Shelby:* I have some information about the show that I think would be valuable to Tommy.
>
> *Stefan* (smirking): Do you?
>
> *Shelby:* There's a notebook—kind of a burn book. I think the producers have used it, and other tactics, to manipulate us.
>
> (Stefan continues to smirk.)
>
> *Shelby:* There's a notebook I brought to Napa with notes on the other contestants. The producers took it when I got here. I think they got one of the other chefs to write really mean things in it and then they planted it for Sophie to find.
>
> (Stefan laughs.)
>
> *Shelby:* I know it sounds crazy, but they asked Dante to spill marinara sauce on Sophie—he told me—so that she would find the notebook they planted in my locker when she borrowed my clean uniform. . . . You don't believe me, do you?

Stefan: I know about the notebook, Shelby.

Shelby (shocked): Well, I'm going to tell Tommy. He deserves to know that people are tampering with his show and exploiting his chefs for the sake of a little cheap drama.

Stcfan: Tommy knows. Whose idea do you think it was?

Shelby: Tommy knows?

Stefan: You can't make an omelet without breaking a few eggs.

As Shelby recounted the exchange, Stan's jaw hung slack. "I knew Stefan was vile, but he really said that? 'You can't make an omelet without breaking a few eggs'?"

Shelby nodded.

"That's so . . . *Days of Our Lives*!" Stan exclaimed, clearly aghast at Stefan's—and Tommy's—machinations. When we thought the MIB had used the burn book to stir up some drama, we hadn't suspected it went all the way to the top.

"*Days of* Our *Lives*," Shelby said. "So much for 'reality.' If they'll admit to planting the notebook to turn us against each other, who knows what else was a setup? Maybe the whole thing is rigged."

We were sitting at our usual table on the dorm patio. If the producers knew that we were onto them, as we were sure Stefan had told them by now, there was no need to hide behind closed doors, walk-in refrigerators, or turned-off mics. We were free to talk. I still couldn't believe it. If the producers were pulling the strings, what else had they done and could they know? Did they know I'd snuck off with Luc? Were they waiting to use it against me? Was Luc part of their plot? I felt sick to my stomach. It was like being trapped in the Fun House of Mirrors at the county fair Alex's family took us to. I didn't know what was real anymore. Had all the blood, sweat, and tears been a total sham? Had I won, or lost, anything honestly?

"Do you think all the tests were fixed?" I asked.

Shelby shrugged. "It's possible. I wouldn't put anything past them now."

Another thought occurred to me. "If they know that we know, do you think that means we can't make it into the finale?"

Shelby shrugged again. "It could go either way. We could blow this thing wide open."

Stan snorted. "Yeah, and have our pants sued off us! We signed a confidentiality agreement, remember?"

Shelby slumped a little. "True."

The three of us sat in silence, undoubtedly all running through our minds anything in the past six weeks that might have been by the producers' design. The limited ingredients, the lack of sleep, the shorter bathroom breaks—suddenly everything seemed part of their scheme. I thought back to comments from the judges, their critiques and praises. Had they really meant any of it?

"Maybe we'll never know," I said, answering my own question out loud.

Stan seemed to puff up a little at this. "It doesn't matter," he said resolutely. "We're good. All of us. Team S is . . .

special, superb, superior. We are a culinary force to be reckoned with. If at least one of us doesn't get to the finale, we can only assume the show is rigged and we're being punished for what we know."

Shelby sat up a little straighter also. "You're right," she said. "I just made quite possibly the world's best profiteroles. I made a bouillabaisse that would have caused Julia Child to weep. We've kicked butt here. If this game is straight, at least one of us will be in the finale."

Choosing to overlook the assumption I knew Shelby was making—that if "one" of Team S made it to the finale, it would be her—I decided to believe what she said. All we had to do was cook food so obviously masterful that even conniving producers couldn't deny us a place in the finale. I thought of my mother's words, the inspiration for Aunt Mary's restaurant: Treat every meal as if it were your last. The idea of a last supper had suddenly taken on a whole new meaning.

FINALE QUALIFIER

Chapter Fourteen

The heat was on. Every week of the show had felt like the hardest yet. Each dish was expected to be the best of our lives thus far. But our weekly tests suddenly seemed like child's play as we prepped for the meal that would send three of us to the finale and five of us away from the NCA for good.

Our slates were clean. This was all that mattered. We needed to knock the judges' socks off. They wanted originality. They wanted a chef who pushed boundaries and fused flavors. They wanted Tommy Chang. They didn't want something you could get at Taverna Ristorante. So I decided to switch gears. I would make salmon *en papillote* (steamed in parchment paper) topped with tomato jam and served with a julienne medley of zucchini, carrots, and turnips in lemon-dill butter.

My salmon would cook quickly, so I had time to focus

on the tomato jam, which was a good thing, because the first batch burned. I blanched the vegetables, submerging them in boiling water for a few seconds and then dipping them in an ice bath to bring out their color. Then I generously seasoned my beautiful fillets with salt and pepper, topped them with a dollop of dill butter and a few slices of lemon, surrounded the fish with the vegetables, and folded the parchment paper into a kind of envelope that would let it all steam. Voilà.

Just as the packets went onto a baking sheet and into the oven, the door to the kitchen opened. In walked none other than Tommy Chang, the man himself, trailed by two cameras. The noisy racket of the kitchen, which I'd learned to tune out, quieted instantly.

Tommy held his hands palms together, namaste-style, in greeting. "Hello, chefs."

"Hello, Chef," some of us parroted back. We were taken off guard by Tommy's sudden flesh-and-blood appearance. Most of us had forgotten the man existed outside of the two-dimensional screen.

"I'm delighted to be back with you at the National Culinary Academy." One camera circled us while another zoomed in on Tommy. "Like every week, you start from scratch. For five of you, this will be your last time in the *Teen Test Kitchen.* Only three of you will return for the live finale. Today, however, we're going to do things a little differently." You could feel the uneasiness settling over the room as he paused. "Normally we have you present your dishes to the judges. This time, they won't know which dish belongs to which chef."

Shelby, Stan, and I looked at each other. We should have known there would be a twist.

They pressure cooked us for three hours. It was the longest we'd ever had to wait for the judges' decision, and it was all the more excruciating because this time we were able to watch from a closed-circuit television as the judges picked apart our dishes both literally and figuratively. It was mortifying. Philip, with his miso-glazed cod with sweet-and-sour cabbage, was the only apparent winner. The other two spots were as up in the air as ever.

We were delirious, spent emotionally and physically. My feet ached, and I was starving. Other than tasting my food as I cooked, I hadn't eaten in six hours. There was a snack table set up by craft service, but I couldn't bring myself to get up to fetch a granola bar. Instead, I sat slumped against a locker, laughing at a joke Stan had made about the glare off Stefan's bald head. Shelby was trying to nap in a chair in the corner. I wished I could sleep.

After what seemed like an eternity, the door to the locker room opened, and we were escorted back to the kitchen. We knew the drill, and we fell into line in front of the judges' table.

"Chefs, welcome back to the Test Kitchen. Judges," Stefan asked, "which dishes passed this test?"

Patricia, Chef Bouchard, and Stefan all looked to Tommy, who was seated in the middle. His face was serious, almost somber, but knowing what I knew about the burn book, it was hard to tell whether this decision truly weighed on him or whether mental anguish just made for good television.

Tommy measured out his words. "Chefs, we'd like to thank you all for your impressive performance today. It seems the National Culinary Academy has taught you well, and we are proud. After a very tough deliberation, we have made our decision. At the top of the class this week are . . . the miso cod, the scallops with celery root puree, and the salmon *en papillote*. If your dish was chosen, please step forward."

I wanted to drop to the floor and cry in relief. I was shaking. Philip, Britney, and I approached the judges' table to the applause of the other chefs. I felt like I was floating.

Each of us identified our dish, and all three judges looked surprised when I claimed the salmon.

Tommy spoke first. "I really enjoyed this dish. It was simple, but it wowed me with its bright, clean flavors. It was a reminder that cooking doesn't have to be complicated to be sophisticated."

"You chose to use a classic French technique," Chef Bouchard said.

"Yes, Chef."

He nodded approvingly.

Patricia chimed in. "Your dish, Sophie, was phenomenal. I'd eat it all over again if I could. I absolutely loved the tomato jam. But . . ."

No, stop, I wanted to say. You can stop right there.

"I don't see you in it," she continued. "Part of what we've hoped to achieve here at *Teen Test Kitchen* is to help you find your own culinary style, to help you define yourself as a chef. This dish, while perfect, just doesn't scream 'Sophie' to me. In fact, I'm still not sure who 'Sophie' is."

Tommy and Chef Bouchard nodded. Stefan sat looking dour as ever. I wasn't sure if or how I was supposed to respond to this alleged identity crisis. "Yes, Chef," I muttered lamely.

"At the finale," Patricia said, and now the word sank in—I had made it to the *finale*!—"I would like to see you, Sophie Nicolaides, teen chef. Can you show us that?"

"Yes, Chef," I replied. I just had to figure out who Sophie Nicolaides, teen chef, was.

"Britney, Philip, Sophie . . . congratulations," said Tommy with a pleased smile. "We'll see you back in the Test Kitchen for the finale."

The other contestants crowded around us. Stan was the first one to me. He squeezed me in a bear hug. "Congratulations, Soph," he said. "You earned it." I turned to look for Shelby as Stan moved on to hug Philip, but I couldn't find her in the swarm. Then I saw her, slipping out the door.

After the hugs and congratulations had been given out and the cameras were turned off, I found her. She was in the locker room. "Shelby," I said into the quiet room. She turned, and I could tell from her red eyes and puffy nose that she'd been crying.

"Congratulations," she said.

"Thanks. Are you okay?"

Shelby forced a smile. "Yeah, yeah. I'm fine," she said, but already the tears had started rolling down her cheeks.

I sat next to her. "I'm sorry you didn't make it to the finale. It's totally bogus. You know if they'd been judging on our whole time here, you would have won. We're not even sure that it's not rigged!"

Shelby quickly wiped at her eyes. "No. No, don't say that. You deserve it, Sophie. And I'm happy for you. I really am."

"I know," I said. And I did know that Shelby was happy for me, as happy for me as I was sad for her.

"You know you have to win now," she said. "For both of us."

"Sure," I said. "Easy as pie."

She smiled. "You might want to leave the pie to me."

Leaving Napa was going to be harder than I had thought it would be. Yes, our cliques had formed quickly and unmistakably. Over seven weeks, we'd rooted for and against each other, advised and teased each other, come through for each other and even deceived each other. We were—always—competitors. But now that we were separating, we were friends too. The eight of us had shared a common experience, one that would forever rank as one of our strangest, most stressful, and most fun. These seven other chefs were the only people in the world who really knew the unreality of this reality experience—not to mention the only ones, legally, I would ever be able to talk about it with. Until the last show aired in November, we were under a strict gag order. I could tell my father about making it to the finale, but that was it. I couldn't even tell my brother or Alex. And I'd only be able to talk to the other chefs after the finale. To avoid potential leaks, we weren't allowed to have any contact until then.

This was what made our good-bye that night on the dorm patio bittersweet. The producers had set up a special farewell dinner for us under the stars. Even the judges and the MIB were there. I knew I'd miss Napa and the beauty of the valley's twisted grapevines spreading out under a bright blue sky. But even more, I'd miss Stan's sense of humor and Shelby's edge. I'd miss Maura's spaciness and Mario's funny laugh and even Dante's quiet swagger. I wondered if I'd get a chance to say good-bye to Luc. I'd seen him only from a distance since the day of our picnic. I was too scared to approach him with cameras around. Perhaps he'd realized what a risk I'd taken that day and didn't want to get me in trouble. That, or he was also part of the producers' master plan, just another plot device. The idea made me angry and slightly nauseated. I put it out of my head.

After dinner, someone had the idea to pass around our chef's jackets for the judges to autograph. And if we were all going to be famous chefs one day, Stan observed, we might as well get each others' autographs too. We knew we had to pack, but we were reluctant to leave the patio. For a moment, the eight cheftestants of *Teen Test Kitchen* stood awkwardly in a circle, no one wanting to be the first to go. Maura, of course, was crying. She and Britney embraced each other tightly; then Mario moved to hug Dante with a macho pat on the back, and we all joined in. We hugged, and we made promises.

"Keep in touch," Maura said as she squeezed my hand.

"I want to come to your restaurant in San Antonio," I told Mario. "And I'll look out for Salsa Mamacita."

This made him happy. "Coming to a grocery store near you!"

Even Philip, Britney, and I hugged, although we knew we'd face each other in three months, adversaries again.

I wished them good luck planning their finale menus. We all wished each other luck. Because we knew that, once the show aired, things would never be the same.

I was talking with Dante about his postshow plans—I wanted to tell him I knew he had meant to spill the marinara sauce on me, but it seemed the moment had passed—when Shelby appeared at my side. "Sophie, I've got to show you something," she whispered.

Her voice was urgent and she seemed agitated, so I excused myself and stepped to the side with her. Shelby held out her autographed apron. Below the *TTK* logo was Stefan's signature in cerulean blue ink. The *a* in his name had the same recognizable tail that we had seen in the burn book.

I looked at her to see if she was saying what I thought she was saying.

"Yep," she said. "Stefan is our culprit."

We'd arrived one by one, and now we would leave the same way. Stan's and Shelby's limos had already taken them to the airport. We'd barely had time even to process Shelby's revelation about Stefan's despicable role in the burn book. Of course, now, it was obvious. Who else would say such spiteful things? Who else would the producers trust with the task? If we'd had another week, I thought, Stan might have hatched a pretty excellent revenge, perhaps involving a dramatic on-camera confrontation. But we didn't have a week. It was time to go.

Maura and I were the last ones left. My limo was ready, but there was some holdup from production, so I waited outside the NCA entrance to lug my suitcase down the same ramp I'd lugged it up seven weeks before. A single camera and sound guy were my audience. They stood chatting, waiting for the word so they could get their shot of me leaving.

Pssst. I heard the sound. It was distinctly a hiss, but I had no idea where it was coming from. *Pssst.* I heard it again. Alarmed, I spun around. "Sophie, here," I heard. Behind the high hedge of bushes that flanked the entrance's handicapped ramp crouched Luc.

"What are you doing?" I asked, confused and amused. The cameraman turned, and I smiled innocently. He went back to talking to the sound guy.

Luc gestured for me to join him behind the bushes. Sensing something was up, the cameraman had his eye on me. In perhaps my most pathetic move to evade the camera yet, I "dropped"—more like tossed—my purse behind the bushes and then went in after it.

I crouched next to Luc. "What are you doing?" I repeated.

"There's something I need to tell you," he whispered.

Luc looked cuter than ever. But this was where he would tell me our whole tryst had been a farce. This was where his conscience would get the better of him, and he would admit that the producers had sent him to flirt for the sake of a better story. I knew it. I braced myself against the sting of those words.

Instead, he kissed me. It was short and light, not much more than a peck, but sweet.

"Sophie?" It was the voice of the production assistant, or assistant producer—I still didn't know the difference.

My head was swimming. "Was there something you needed to tell me?" I asked.

Luc smiled. "No. That was it." I could have melted like a Popsicle on a hot day.

"Sophie?" the voice repeated.

I kissed him this time.

Then before he could respond, I said, "Got it!" Quickly I popped up from behind the bushes, clutching my purse.

Megan and the cameraman looked at me as if I'd finally been driven mad. She listened into her earpiece. "Copy," she said to her headset. "We're a go." Then to me, "We're going to have you step inside, so we can get a shot of you coming out of the big doors and down to the car."

I nodded and took the handle of my roller bag, wishing I could stop time for just a few more seconds with Luc. I glanced quickly back at him, still squatting on his heels behind the bushes. He grinned and waved, but I couldn't give away his position. So I said, "Thank you," and hoped he knew I intended it for him.

Chapter Fifteen

Sometimes sleeping in your own bed feels strange. The first two weeks back home after the show, I kept waking up and expecting to see Shelby's bunk above me. I kept dreaming about the Test Kitchen, too. There would be a moment of alarm when I woke, my dreams still fading, where I panicked that the stove was broken or my rice was burning.

Dad, Raffi, and Alex had picked me up at the airport. Alex and Raffi held a WELCOME HOME banner. It had felt better to hug them than it ever had before. They were full of questions—most of them ones they knew I couldn't answer.

School started a week after I returned from Napa. It seemed most of Lakeview High School, students and teachers included, knew I'd been on a reality show over the summer. When they peppered me with questions and got few answers, though, it eventually became old news. The first episode hadn't yet aired.

Life got back to normal. It was as if Napa had been a dream. Alex and I dropped into our old routine. We met at my locker every morning and IM'd almost every night. It turned out I hadn't had to worry about Lindy at all. She had started dating Will Frances the day after I left for California. My feelings for Alex, however, were as confusing as the day I'd left. I considered telling him about Luc but decided against it, not sure why. I mentioned the postcard, telling him how much I had needed it at the time. He told me he'd picked it out, remembering how much I loved the cherry blossoms, but didn't say anything about the word on it that had rattled me most: *love.*

The only thing that felt different was the restaurant. The kitchen at Taverna Ristorante had never seemed shabby before. But after almost two months of working with world-class chefs in a state-of-the-art kitchen and with food so fresh you could still smell the sun and dirt on it, this felt like the afternoon shift at Burger King.

"Have you thought about using organic chicken?" I asked my father one day as we unloaded a shipment of the frozen and no doubt preservative-laden breasts we'd always used.

"Sure," my father replied without pausing from the unloading. "But I've also thought about sending you to college. Organic is expensive." That was the end of that conversation.

One unusually busy Wednesday evening, one of the burners on the stove went out as I was in the middle of searing a pork chop. "Ugh! How do you work here?" I balked. Luís moved the pan to another burner and raised an eyebrow. "I manage," he said.

I mentioned sous-vide once, a technique all the big

chefs were using that involved cooking vacuum-sealed foods at low temperatures for extended periods of time. We'd tried it on *Teen Test Kitchen*, and the flavor and texture it produced were unquestionably better than conventional cooking methods. My father looked at me like I was crazy. "You want to vacuum your food? What are you, an astronaut now?" he said. I didn't have the energy to explain that I hadn't meant freeze-dried.

On Saturday night, a few weeks after coming home, I couldn't muster an appetite for our normal family dinner at the restaurant.

"What's wrong?" Alex asked. I had pushed my calamari around my plate and had barely touched my baked penne.

Slumped in my chair, I picked at it with a fork. "The calamari is chewy and needs more acid, and the penne is dried out. There's just no creativity in it."

"It tasted pretty good to me," Alex said.

I was frustrated, and I supposed it was beginning to show. But I felt like I'd been shown the Sistine Chapel and then brought back to finger painting, unable to tell anyone what I'd seen.

Our third week back at school, though, everything changed. My father decided to host a viewing party at the restaurant for *Teen Test Kitchen*'s premiere. He invited every customer we had that week, as well as the staff and any lucky delivery driver who happened to be around. Alex and his family came, along with a few other kids we hung out with at school. Raffi also brought two friends. It was the entirety of my social life in one room.

My father lugged an old TV set down from the office—the kind that was as deep as it was wide and weighed two hundred pounds. Nonna had made platters of baklava and koulourakia cookies, and my father passed out glasses of prosecco and ouzo for the adults and sparkling grape juice for the kids. As eight o'clock neared, we gathered around the old TV set. Everyone was excited but me. I felt like I might be sick from nerves.

Raffi lowered the lights as the show's theme music, a generic pop-rock riff I'd never heard before, started. The show's logo splashed across the screen.

Alex grinned at me. "Ready for your close-up?"

The screen flashed images of each of the chefs—Mario with a bead of sweat dripping down his face, Britney selecting produce at the farmer's market, Shelby tossing shrimp in a pan, me stomping grapes at the vineyard—and finished with the promo shots we'd taken the first day. Mario crossed his arms menacingly. Stan had a huge grin on his face. Britney actually winked. "You didn't mention there was a hot one!" Raffi said.

When my face appeared on the screen, the room erupted in applause and cheers. My father patted me proudly on the back. I buried my face in my hands.

"I look fat!" I protested.

"The camera adds ten pounds," Raffi said.

"Shhh, Raffi," Nonna hissed. "Sophia, you look beautiful," she said, stroking my hair.

My initial days in Napa came flooding back to me, only the events played out on-screen in a much neater, more organized, and admittedly more exciting progression than my memories. Things were spliced and edited and packaged. It was like *My Life: The Director's Cut.* There we were getting out of our limos (thankfully, they omitted my collision course with the light boom); there were the judges filing into the kitchen; there was a close-up on Tommy Chang introducing them. The events of the first week unfolded in an hour, counting commercial breaks with ads for spaghetti sauce and garbage bags. The episode covered our lessons, labs, and finally our test, interspersed with clips from our Kitchen Confidentials and some "get to know us" footage shot during the little downtime we did have.

It was hard to remember sometimes that it was actually me on-screen, that those were my experiences. Some things I didn't remember the way they were shown, like Philip looking so smug after his win. There was a conversation the eight of us had about being intimidated by Stefan that came out sounding like we were talking about Tommy. They used a clip from one of my Kitchen Confidentials that was filmed much later in the show, the third or fourth week at least. This was reality TV, but for me, it was supremely surreal.

In the scenes from "next week," there was a shot of me leaning on one of the worktables in the kitchen, shooting what looked like a death stare at Shelby.

"Whoa!" Raffi said. "What'd she do to piss you off?"

"Nothing! Shelby's my friend." I remembered that day. I wasn't glaring at Shelby; I was planning what would become my failed eggs Benedict.

"So what'd you think?" I asked Alex later, once

everyone had emptied out of the restaurant, congratulating me and saying things like, "I've never known someone famous before!" My father and Raffi were lugging the TV back up to the office.

Alex's hands were stuffed into his pockets, and his bangs, longer than ever, had fallen into his eyes. He flipped them aside with a nervous flick of his head. "It was cool," he said.

"That's it?"

"I mean, it's weird to see you on TV, ya know?"

I gnawed mercilessly at my fingernail. "Yeah, I know."

"But it's good. This is gonna be big, Sophie."

I managed a smile, but my heart was sinking. From what I'd seen and what I knew, this might be big, but it was not going to be good. More than ever, I was at the mercy of *Teen Test Kitchen*.

By the next morning at school, interest in the show had been renewed. My popularity had rocketed to new levels. People I didn't know were saying hi to me in the halls. Two freshmen asked me for my autograph.

Between third and fourth period, I was standing at my locker when I heard a voice behind me say, "Hey." I turned to find Ava Griffin, the closest thing to a Queen Bee Lakeview High School had. Her friend and sidekick, Emma Brewer, an only slightly less powerful clone of Ava, was standing behind her.

"I saw you on TV," Ava said. I crammed my Spanish workbook into my locker and extracted my history binder. "You're, like, a chef, right?" she asked.

"Yeah. Something like that."

"Doesn't your family have a restaurant in Georgetown?"

"Yeah."

"I thought so. My parents make us go there sometimes."

My cheeks burned, but not at the snobbish tone in Ava's voice. I blushed because, for the first time ever, I was embarrassed—not that my family ran a restaurant, which in my book was awesome, but that the restaurant was Taverna Ristorante, a place with a kids' menu and cheap posters of the Acropolis on the walls. It was hardly the Michelin-starred restaurant I dreamed of and actually saw myself in.

"Do you work there?" Ava asked.

"Not really," I lied. "I'm gonna start my own restaurant one day. Probably in New York or California."

"Oh," Ava said lazily. "That's cool. So did you win?"

"I can't talk about it."

Ava looked put out by this. "Why not?"

"Because I signed a contract that said I couldn't."

"What would they do to you?" Emma asked. I could see a whitish-blue wad of gum in her cheek, even though we weren't supposed to chew gum on school property.

"I don't know," I answered. "Probably sue me."

The bell rang for fourth period. "See ya," Ava said, and the two girls walked away.

"So I guess you're free Saturday night then?" It was Alex's voice behind me.

I turned, surprised to find him leaning on the locker next to mine. I hadn't heard him come up. "No. We're open Saturday. What do you mean?"

"Nothing," he said, obviously irritated. "I'll see you later."

Something was off with Alex recently. This wasn't the first time he'd been short with me since I got home, and I'd noticed he was logging off our ichats earlier and earlier each night, saying he had to do homework or help his mom. But the flan didn't really hit the fan until the second episode—and the Donut Den comment.

I was home. My father and Raffi were at the restaurant; they'd started recording the show, since they couldn't miss Friday night dinner service every week. Alex was babysitting his little sister, so Nonna and Pappou were my company for the evening. Pappou had fallen asleep shortly after the first commercial break. I tried not to take it personally; he fell asleep during every show.

It was our French week, and when the screen filled with an image of me on our trip to the vineyard, practically salivating over Luc, I cringed.

"Who is that boy?" Nonna asked, her interest suddenly piqued. She stopped her sock darning for one second. My father had begged Nonna to just let him buy Pappou new socks, but Nonna wouldn't hear of it.

"He's a student at the school. His father owns the vineyard we visited."

Nonna just nodded, but her gaze didn't leave the television after that, even as she darned. The camera didn't let up either. Later in the episode, there was a long view of my eyes following Luc as he crossed the cafeteria. I prayed that in California he was too busy cooking or grape stomping to watch the show.

It wasn't until a scene almost at the end of the episode, where Shelby and Stan were grilling me at lunch about Luc, that I realized what was coming. I remembered our conversation. I hadn't remembered we were on mic.

"I'm trying to figure out which one is more your type, Alex or Luc," the TV Shelby said.

I jumped up from the couch, knowing what was coming next. "Oh, no! Oh, no! Oh, no!" I cried, gripping both sides of the television, willing the screen to go black, the power grid to go down, satellites to explode.

"I mean, it's like burgers versus coq au vin, the Donut Den versus . . . Le Bernardin," the Sophie on the screen answered, as a little piece of the real Sophie died.

The cameras had been so far away, and I still hadn't gotten used to the idea that I was almost always mic'ed. It was just lunchtime talk, nothing to do with the competition or the show. But when we were on *TTK*, everything had to do with the show.

After four phone calls, two text messages, and a voice mail, I was officially stalking Alex. His silence was anything but a good sign. I went to his house the next afternoon. He was in his yard, fixing the chain on his bike.

He didn't look up as I got out of my dad's car and walked to where he was kneeling, wrenching away at a bolt. "Hey," I said.

"The Donut Den, huh?"

"I'm sorry, Alex. That came out all wrong. I told you they're totally twisting our words. They're taking things out of context."

"In what context is being compared to the Donut Den a good thing?"

"I know it sounded weird. I just meant you're, like, my comfort food, and Luc is . . ."

"Luc is what? Fine dining? I get it." He started to climb onto his bike. "Glad to know you think so highly of me."

"Alex, wait," I pleaded. "You have to trust me. You know me. You know I'm not the person they're portraying me to be."

"I don't know if I know who you are anymore, Sophie. It's not just the show, it's you. You think you're all hot snot and booger balls. You're not the person you were before you left."

The mixture of anger and distrust on Alex's face made my heart hurt. The fact that even when mad at me he still used our old childhood insult only made it worse.

"What happened on that show?" he asked earnestly.

I thought the question was rhetorical, but he waited for me to respond. "Do you mean really what happened?" I asked. "You know I can't tell you, Alex. At least not until it's over." He was my best friend, but the show lawyers had warned us in our media training that the nondisclosure clause in our contract was serious.

"Right," Alex said. He stepped on the pedal and rode away without as much as a backward glance. Watching him go felt like getting the wind knocked out of me.

The shows kept airing every Friday night at eight and rerunning through the week like the sting after the face slap. It didn't take long for the characters the producers had picked for us to emerge. With just a little creative editing and selective storytelling, it became clear that what Stan and Shelby had joked about our first night on the dorm patio was true. Each chef had been selected to play a role in the reality show formula. Every good story had its villains and its heroes, and apparently *TTK* was no exception. We weren't contestants, we were caricatures, not even of ourselves but of some stereotype the producers had seen in us.

Sure, Stan was gay and not afraid to show it, but on the show, he was one step from dressing as Liza Minnelli and singing "New York, New York." Shelby was competitive, no doubt about it. Her single-mindedness had nearly driven me over the edge at times. But on the show, she was portrayed as a cutthroat, take-no-prisoners bitch. Dante had always been the quiet type, even the quiet type who would spill marinara on me at a producer's orders, but with their ominous cuts and clever editing, he was the silent menace. The friction between Philip and Shelby was elevated into a full-blown feud that looked like it almost tore the show apart.

They showed my visits with Aunt Mary and a few more times hinted at my flirtation with Luc, but to my amazement, they never showed or talked about the burn book, though they milked every suspicious glance and every stolen whisper they could out of the situation around it. Shelby and I were the show "frenemies." In my Kitchen Confidential, the one after I'd found the burn book and the MIB was pushing me to talk about Shelby, they cobbled together my words to make it sound like I was calling Shelby "funny" (not in the flattering way) and "competitive." "Shelby just really wants to win," I said into the camera.

Edit, edit, edit. "Some people have surprised me." None of the nice things I said when sidestepping the MIB's questions made it in. It looked like I was trashing her.

I was horrified. Viewers, though, were eating it up. I didn't care as much as Raffi did. I could barely watch the show anymore, but he e-mailed me articles, the number of views on YouTube, blog comments both positive and bitterly negative (and I knew he was filtering the worst of it). He Googled my name every day until I was the first hit; it took twelve days.

At the restaurant, I was shocked at the number of people who came in looking for me. At first the waitstaff loved it—more business meant more tips. Then word got out, and every table was holding them up, asking about me, wondering if I could come out to take a picture with them. If I had wanted the attention, it would have been flattering, even fun. But this wasn't the kind of attention I was looking for. I wanted my food to make me famous, not the character I had, apparently, played on TV.

The worst of it, though, was the irony of having so many people I didn't even know interested, dying to hear anything and everything, and yet having no one I could really talk to. I thought of that line from the poem we'd studied the year before, *The Rime of the Ancient Mariner*: "Water, water, everywhere, Nor any drop to drink." Now I knew how Coleridge's sailors felt.

For almost five weeks, Alex and I had been like strangers. After the Donut Den debacle, I'd apologized as much as I knew how. He said he accepted my apology but started making up excuses for why he couldn't hang out, until finally I gave up. Part of me had to wonder if he was just angry, or if Shelby's hinting at a romantic relationship between us on national television had freaked him out. I didn't know which reason for avoiding me would be worse.

My father was crazy busy at the restaurant, and I couldn't trust Raffi, with the way he was obsessing about the show. If he slipped up and told someone else who told someone else, I would be in serious trouble. It was better not to talk about it at all. So I locked the experience away in a box and let the show speak for itself.

I couldn't even call Shelby to explain when and how those comments about her had been made, or Stan. I was living in a deep, dark well of secrecy and suspicion. The only light I could see, my only chance at redemption, was the finale. Until then, all I would let myself focus on was my menu. Three courses, one chance.

Lobster Ravioli with Champagne Cream Sauce

When I was packing for California, I came across my mother's recipe for lobster ravioli. I don't know when she made it—maybe it was for a special dinner with my dad or a staff meal at Taverna Ristorante—but I knew I should remember it, just in case. Good thing I did, because pairing her recipe with a champagne cream sauce I came up with (Napa Valley champagne, of course) was the perfect way to go into the finale. I made my own pasta (hey, it's in my blood), but you can also use wonton wrappers from the grocery store for a super easy shortcut.

SERVES 4

Ingredients

For the Lobster Ravioli

2 pounds fresh lobster meat, cooked

1 cup crème fraîche (or sour cream)

Kosher salt and freshly ground black pepper to taste

1 egg

32 wonton wrappers

For the Champagne Cream Sauce

½ stick (¼ cup) unsalted butter

1 shallot, minced

1 cup champagne or other sparkling white wine
½ cup heavy cream
2 tablespoons fresh tarragon, finely chopped
Kosher salt and freshly ground black pepper to taste

Directions

1. Assemble the ravioli: In a mixing bowl, combine the lobster meat, crème fraîche, and salt and pepper using your hands. Set the bowl aside in the refrigerator.

2. Beat the egg, then add a little water to it to make an egg wash. Place 16 wonton wrappers in front of you. (They stick together, so make sure you've peeled them apart well.) Brush egg wash all around the edges of the wrappers. Drop a large spoonful of lobster filling onto the center of each wrapper. Top it with a second wrapper, and use your fingers to press around the filling and seal the wrappers together. Place raviolis on a cookie sheet lined with wax paper or parchment, cover them with plastic wrap, and refrigerate them until needed (you can make these a few hours in advance).

3. To make the sauce, melt the butter in a large sauté pan over medium heat. Add the shallot and cook, stirring, for 3 minutes. Remove the pan from the heat and carefully add the champagne, then return the pan to the heat and bring it to a boil (don't let the champagne boil

over the sides; reduce the heat if needed). Add the cream and tarragon, season the mixture with salt and pepper, and stir well. Let the sauce simmer until it is slightly reduced and thickened, about 5 minutes.

4. Bring a pot of salted water to a gentle boil. Carefully place half of the raviolis in the pot and cook them until they rise to the surface and float. Use a slotted spoon to transfer the cooked raviolis from the pot to a serving dish. Repeat the process with the remaining raviolis, then top them with champagne cream sauce and serve.

THE FINALE

Chapter Sixteen

The last show aired the first Friday in November. I called Aunt Mary the next day. There was a one-week break, then a *Teen Test Kitchen* special on the judges and the NCA, then the finale, with the winner announced live. That meant almost three weeks still to plan and practice my meal. I wanted Aunt Mary's advice.

Patricia's words at the last challenge had hit me hard twice—the first time in Napa and the second time when I heard them on television: "I would like to see you, Sophie Nicolaides, teen chef. Can you show us that?" I wasn't sure. Could I? Did I even know what that meant?

Aunt Mary had a way of asking questions, not answering them. She didn't tell me what to make, but somehow, by the end of our conversation, I knew my menu. What was more important, I felt it lived up to the demand Patricia had made. This menu was me.

The night before I flew back to Napa, I lay awake thinking about all the things that had changed since I walked into that hotel ballroom with Alex by my side and without a broiler pan. For one, Alex was no longer by my side. I wanted to blame the producers, and in some ways I did. But really, who could I blame but myself? Yes, the producers had edited to suit their own needs, but the truth was, nothing they'd shown had been made up. I'd said it and done it. They had it on tape. All I could hope was that Alex would forgive me, would recognize the stress I had been under, and would let me back into his life, even just as a friend.

While I worried I might have lost one friend, I also desperately hoped I still had two more: Stan and Shelby. They'd said some cutting things also, of course, but I knew they were edited the same as I was. Did they realize that too? After everything we'd been through, did they trust me?

Yet behind it all—the frustration and sense of betrayal over my portrayal on the show, the irony that my life was suddenly public but more lonely than ever, the fear that none of my friends would ever speak to me again—was also a new self-confidence. I had gone to Napa the first time as a cook. I was returning as a chef. And I was about to prove it.

The Test Kitchen was just as we left it. Even Patricia, Chef Bouchard, and Stefan, whom I could barely look at without disgust, were in their usual places at the judges' table. Tommy, who'd somehow found a way to make it to his own show's finale, greeted us. "Chefs, welcome back to *Teen Test Kitchen*," he said as Philip, Britney, and I lined up in front of them.

They looked good. Britney, to my surprise, had gone

brunette. Philip had new glasses and was definitely now wearing product in his hair. I wondered if I'd missed the makeover memo.

"For your final test, you will have one day to prep and one day to cook your three-course menu. You'll need it. This time, you're not just serving the judges; you're also serving twenty faculty and students at the National Culinary Academy. The judges will take into account their comments as they decide the winner of *Teen Test Kitchen.*"

This twist, news to us, set off a panic that I could feel ripple through Philip and Britney as well. We'd presented, at most, five versions of our dishes before: one for each of the judges and Stefan and one for photography. You could burn a tray of toast, but as long as you had five acceptable pieces, you were fine. To execute my meal for twenty-five people at the level of precision I knew I needed to win would indeed be a test.

Tommy continued. "To help you, you will each get one assistant. Chefs, meet your sous-chefs."

Through the door walked Mario, Dante, Maura, Shelby, and Stan. Philip, Britney, and I jumped up and down in surprise and gratitude. I could have cried with relief. There was no group of people I would have rather seen at that moment. Shelby looked exactly the same, tall and thin, though her face was a little rounder, healthier. Stan had lost weight. He winked at me and turned sideways to flaunt his new figure like a pinup model.

We each got to pick one sous-chef. Philip drew the longest straw and selected Stan. Britney, no surprise, went with Maura.

"I pick Shelby," I said.

She came to stand beside me.

"You're not mad at me?" I asked.

Shelby looked surprised that I would ask. "For what? The stuff you said in your Kitchen Confidentials?" She laughed. "It was all true!" She hooked her arm through mine. "Let's kick Stan's scrawny butt."

"Very well," said Tommy. "In a moment, we will let you confer with your sous-chefs on your menu. But first we have one more twist. The two remaining chefs . . ." Tommy nodded at Dante and Mario, who were still standing where they'd come in the door, "will be on the judges' panel."

Shelby's face went pale. Our guest judges were hardly impartial.

Shelby loved my menu. It started with lobster ravioli, a recipe I'd unearthed in my mother's handwritten card catalog, in a champagne cream sauce, my own addition. It progressed with herb-encrusted lamb, the same dish that had gotten me on *TTK* in the first place, this time paired with pan-fried potato gnocchi in a wild mushroom sauce. It concluded with deconstructed baklava: honey ice cream with pistachio brittle in a phyllo cup. It was a decadent bill of fare.

I'd practiced the recipes at home at least half a dozen times, my father grumbling each time at the cost of lobster, though never complaining when he sat down to eat it. I probably could have made this meal with my eyes closed, but I'd learned my lesson about expressing that sentiment.

Prep day in the kitchen was festive. We talked as we

worked, sharing stories about what had happened to us since returning home from the show. *The San Francisco Bay Guardian* had done a cover story on Philip. Britney had gotten a new boyfriend and already broken up with him, something I knew would cheer Mario, who had come back to Napa with a tattoo of the *TTK* logo on his forearm. Stan and Shelby were both looking to apply to another prestigious culinary school in New York, a plan they'd hatched together our last night in Napa. They were saving an application with my name on it, just in case I didn't win the scholarship to the NCA. Maura said her life hadn't changed too much, although people occasionally recognized her in the grocery store. It felt like a happy reunion and a chance to catch up and—finally—talk openly about our experiences. It wasn't until the next day, when the big red clock started ticking, that things got hairy.

When I brought my pot to the kitchen's large sink to fill it for my gnocchi, I found Stan and Philip were standing over it. Stan was making a fuss about something.

"What's wrong?" I asked.

Philip was running his hand under the cold water. "Nothing," he answered quickly.

"He burned his hand," Stan said. "Philip, you should get the doctor to look at it."

"I said I'm fine!" Philip huffed. But he uncovered his palm, and I saw the red welt already starting to rise and blister.

I winced. "Philip, you really should get it looked at."

"That's it," Stan said, starting to get flustered now. "I'm

getting the medic. Medic! Medic!" he shouted toward a production assistant. The guy came running.

Philip sheepishly used his good hand to push his glasses, which had slipped, back onto his nose. Two cameramen raced to get a shot of Philip's hand as the doctor on call pushed through to examine him. It was a second-degree burn, he said, pressing lightly with a gloved finger around Philip's wound. Philip flinched in pain.

"Do you want to finish?" the MIB asked. "You can quit if you need to. But you'll forfeit." He had not changed a bit.

Philip set his jaw. "No," he said dramatically. "I'll finish."

Stan beamed with pride. They bandaged Philip's hand, covered it in a latex glove, and we all pressed on. Thirty minutes on the clock.

"How's the pistachio brittle?" I asked Shelby. With her dessert expertise, she wanted to make that part of the baklava herself. She was cracking pieces off the sheet of golden, glassy candy.

"Good, Chef," she addressed me, without thinking. I laughed.

The lobster ravioli were filled and ready to boil. The phyllo cups I'd prepared the day before. The ice cream was still freezing up. The lamb was ready to go in the broiler. The dried mushrooms were reconstituting in water, and the gnocchi just needed to be pan-fried. I looked around. How was I doing? Okay. There were twenty-six hungry diners outside, but still twenty minutes on the clock.

"Shelby," I said when the mushrooms were nice and tender and simmering in the saucepan, "I'm gonna start plating the ravioli."

"Yes, Chef," she said, intentionally this time. She was arranging the phyllo cups on their individual dishes.

I'd gotten all but three ravioli on plates when Shelby rushed up to me. "Where's the champagne cream sauce?"

My heart stopped. "I thought you made it," I said.

Her eyes went wide as she shook her head. "I thought you did."

"Crap!" There were nine minutes on the clock, and when it reached zero, our first course was going out whether we were ready or not.

I raced to the stovetop and slammed down a saucepan. In went the minced shallots and champagne. "Come on, come on," I coaxed, begging the mixture to boil. There were five minutes and fifteen seconds left on the clock.

"How's the lamb?" I asked. The staggered courses were really throwing me off. It was like having three giant clocks ticking down instead of one.

"Great," she said. "It should be ready to plate just in time."

"Thank you." I realized it was the first time I'd said it all day. A moment of clarity. I looked at Shelby. "Really, thank you."

"Don't mention it," she said. "Ooh. I think it's reduced."

"Cream," I said.

Shelby handed me the cream, like a nurse handing off a scalpel to a surgeon. I dumped it in and turned down the heat.

"Let me stir while you check everything else," Shelby said. The sauce had to reduce more.

I handed over the spatula. The lamb, in the oven, looked

good. I just hoped all twenty-six chops were cooking evenly. I was happy with the pistachio brittle but prayed the ice cream wouldn't melt under the hot television lights. The ravioli were hot but needed their sauce, or they'd soon cool to a gluey mess.

I went back to check on Shelby. There was one minute and twenty seconds on the clock. Philip and Stan were running around like chickens with their heads cut off, but Britney and Maura were finished. They were watching us and watching the clock tick down.

Shelby ground some fresh black pepper into the saucepan, and I tasted. "Hoh, hoh, hoh!" I panted, the sauce burning my mouth. It was definitely thinner than I would have liked, but it had to go now or never. The numbers above Britney's head were ticking fast. "How am I going to plate it in time?"

"Forty-five seconds!" Stan yelled.

Britney didn't hesitate. "We'll help," she said. She grabbed a clean pot, poured half the sauce into it, and started down my line of plates, ladling the sauce over the ravioli. Shelby grabbed another spoon, then Maura, and in seconds, all of us were ladling like maniacs.

"Three, two, one!" Stan called.

Everyone threw up their hands. Shelby had gotten to the last ravioli just in time.

Our meals were served course by course in the NCA's formal dining room. The judges, including Mario and Dante, sat at the head table. Each time I was called from the kitchen to present my dish, I scanned the crowd, hoping Luc might be among the student diners. All I saw was a sea of unfamiliar and expectant faces.

We had reached dessert, and judging from the empty plates, my pistachio brittle had been a hit, but the ice cream had in fact melted under the lights. I hated to think what the puddle of honey-flavored ice cream soup had done to the crispy phyllo.

"Sophie," Tommy said when I was called to the judges' table, "tell us about your meal."

I took a deep breath and prepared to do a verbal tap dance. "Patricia said she wanted to see *me* in my food. I think that's been the hardest thing for me here—figuring out what that means. I grew up with Mediterranean flavors, so they're part of who I am. But something I've loved about my experience here has been the focus on fresh, local ingredients. A friend once told me to respect your food, and it will tell you what to make. I think that's also part of who I am now."

Patricia smiled. "Thank you, Sophie."

"Is there anything in particular you worked on while you were at home?" Chef Bouchard asked.

I looked directly at Stefan as I answered. "Well, Stefan let me know that my plating was sometimes sloppy and that I have a tendency to overseason, so I was aware of those two things. I also wanted to show something a little more sophisticated with my dessert, which was how I came up with the idea to deconstruct the traditional baklava."

Stefan's face hardened as I repeated verbatim his criticisms from the burn book. His eyebrow twitched almost imperceptibly. I wanted him to know that he could say many things about us, but he couldn't say that we hadn't cooked our hearts out. I had been amazed at what I saw come out of the kitchen that night, and proud—of all of us. I couldn't imagine that the comment cards from the NCA students and staff now stacked in front of the judges weren't filled with glowing reviews.

Once Britney and Philip had also been cross-examined, the judges excused us to the Pressure Cooker, one place in Napa I hadn't missed. Shelby high-fived me as I came in. Stan was beside himself over the way I'd skewered Stefan in front of everyone. He said he'd watched the MIB's face redden as he realized I was quoting the burn book. I had to admit it had felt good.

My nerves were jangled, but an eerie calm came over me when the PA finally called us back into the Test Kitchen. This was it.

The judges looked solemn but sure. Tommy addressed us for the last time. "Chefs, your meals were fantastic. You have all exhibited a talent, technique, and dedication to the culinary arts that goes far beyond your years. I would be honored to have any of you in my kitchen."

By now I knew there was always a *but.*

"But," Tommy continued, "there can be only one chef at the top of this class. The judges have agreed"—he looked back at Dante and Mario, who nodded—"that the winner of *Teen Test Kitchen* and the recipient of a scholarship to the National Culinary Academy and an internship at my New York City restaurant, Om, is . . ."

Time seemed to stop. It was almost over.

"Philip."

The now-familiar *TTK* theme song suddenly blared from unseen speakers. Confetti and balloons released from the ceiling, showering us as we all clapped for Philip. Britney and I hugged him and then hugged each other. What we weren't expecting, however, was to hug our families. The doors to the dining room opened, and in came a group of people I knew immediately to be my competitors' parents. Philip's dad looked exactly like him, down to the glasses he wore. Britney's little golden-haired brothers raced toward her. And at the back of the pack was my father, my brother, Aunt Mary . . . and Alex.

"What? What . . . ?" was all I could manage as I rushed to them, laughing.

My father, with tears in his eyes, threw his arms around me. "I am so proud of you, Sophia," he said into my hair as he embraced me. "So proud of you." And it felt so good to hear.

I finally got my voice back as my brother came in for a hug. "What are you doing here?"

"The show flew us out! Pretty sweet, huh?" said Raffi.

I was still in disbelief. My aunt smiled and stretched out her arms. "Good job, sweetie," she said as I gravitated into them. "Your mother would be so proud of you." Those words were better than winning.

And then there was Alex. "Can I?" he asked, awkwardly reaching for a hug.

"Of course," I said.

It felt strange to be in his arms but also just right. Now that he was back, I didn't want to let go. I looked at him, relieved but questioning, when I finally pulled back. What had happened to make him forgive me?

"Stan called me," he said, then quickly looked around to make sure no producers or crew were nearby. He continued in a lower voice. "He called me a few days ago and told me I should come out, that you'd want me here. He said the way the show portrayed some things really wasn't truthful—something about a burn book?"

Stan to the rescue—of course. He knew he could get in trouble for doing it. I wondered how he'd even found Alex's number.

My father and aunt had stepped away to talk to some of the other parents and chefs. Raffi, of course, had found Britney. Alex continued. "I realized if he was willing to take the risk to call me, then he did know the real you. I'm sorry I doubted you, Soph. It was just hard to hear some of that stuff because . . ." Alex seemed to struggle for words. "I like you, Sophie. Like, like-like you."

"I liked you first!" I blurted.

Alex seemed surprised. We both burst out laughing. "Really?" we said at the same time.

"Maybe we could hang out when we get back? You know, like, a real date or something," Alex said, suddenly bashful. I had never seen him that way before.

I realized Alex was not the kind of guy who would take me on a blindfolded picnic in the Napa countryside. I knew that, but I liked him not in spite of it but because of it. He knew me better than anyone in the world. "I have the perfect place in mind," I said.

"The Donut Den?" he asked, laughing.

"They do have the best powdered doughnuts in town. . . ."

Shelby and Stan found us, and Alex excused himself,

letting us have a moment. He put a hand on Stan's shoulder as he walked away. "Thanks, man," he said. Stan made a tiny curtsy.

"Hey," he said to me with puppy-dog eyes. "How are you?"

"I'm fine," I said. "Really."

"You know, I've been thinking about it," said Shelby, "and I'm still not so sure the producers—"

I stopped her before she could say anything more. "I don't even care anymore. Rigged or not, I think the right person won. Philip is a phenomenal chef."

Stan looked grateful to hear me say it. "I'm just sorry I couldn't help you more," said Shelby.

"Please! I couldn't have put out a single dish without you. And don't be sorry. I'm not. To be honest, I'm not so sure I'd want to be Tommy Chang's protégé. I think I may have found another mentor."

Stan raised an eyebrow. "Luc?" he whispered salaciously.

"No! Geez, Stan. It's a one-track mind in there. I meant my aunt. She said if I wanted, I could work at the Last Supper next summer. . . . But, speaking of Luc, you guys haven't seen him, have you?" I asked.

"Of course," Shelby said. "He's over there."

I turned to where Shelby nodded. Luc was standing beyond the television cameras, in the shadows against the back wall of the dining room. He waved. "Go ahead," said Stan. I glanced at Alex. He was being introduced to the judges by my aunt.

Luc and I met just outside the circle of crew celebrating a job finished. "Congratulations," he said to me.

"I didn't win."

"Are you sure?" he asked. "I think you all did." I smiled. He was right.

Luc's expression suddenly became more serious. "Sophie, I feel I should say something. I didn't come to the NCA to be on television," he said. "I came here because I love to cook."

My heart sank. "I know," I said. "Luc, I'm so sorry for anything I said on camera that may have dragged you into it. A lot of it—"

He stopped me. "I was going to say I know you were here for the same reason. You are talented, Sophie. Really. I hope you see that. And you stayed true to yourself. That is the most important test of a chef."

"Thank you."

"You are welcome," he said, not breaking his gaze from mine.

"So you only have a semester left. Where will you go next?" I asked.

"To New York! There is a restaurant that has offered me a job—just as a commis, but it's a start."

"Wow. New York."

"Any time you want to come, I hope you will look me up."

"I will," I promised. I had always wanted to see New York. For now, though, I was happy where I was. Le Bernardin could wait; I had a hankering for the Donut Den.

My father couldn't help himself. When Aunt Mary wasn't looking, he dumped three more cloves of garlic into the pot of Tuscan white bean soup simmering on the stove. We were celebrating with our own wrap party at the Last Supper.

Despite his preconceived notions, my father was impressed. "It's very nice," he said, patting one of the thick wood columns in the middle of the dining room.

"Okay!" Aunt Mary called, coming back in from the garden with a bunch of fresh basil. "Everyone grab a bowl. We're doing this family style tonight."

She directed us each to a seat around the long table. Shelby and Stan sat on one side of me, Alex on the other.

"So, Sophie, what are you going to do now?" Aunt Mary asked as she passed the bread.

"Finish high school?" I joked.

"You bet your bippy," my father piped from his end of the table.

Alex prodded me with his elbow. "But tell them what you want to do later."

"You mean the restaurant?"

"You want to open a restaurant?" my aunt asked, delighted. "That's great, Sophie."

"That's what she's going to call it: Sophie," Alex said.

"Actually, I think I've changed my mind."

"No restaurant?" my father asked.

"No, I'll have a restaurant one day. But I'm going to call it Sophia."

My father beamed and raised his glass of Clos d'Été. "That, I can toast to."

"*Thavma!*" Alex exclaimed. He raised his glass with one hand and took mine in his other. I squeezed it as we all clinked our glasses together. Looking down the table at my family and friends, new and old, I felt life was marvelous, even miraculous. "*Thavma!*" I toasted. "And *buon appetito*!"

Deconstructed Baklava

The finale to my finale! I wanted to honor my Mediterranean roots but prove to the judges that I could make a classic my own. This dessert incorporates all the flavors and textures of baklava in a playful, modern update. It takes a lot of work, but all three parts can be made in advance, so it's easier than you think to make for a special dinner.

SERVES 4

Ingredients

For the Honey Ice Cream

2 cups heavy cream

1 cup half-and-half

2/3 cup honey

2 eggs

A pinch of kosher salt

For the Phyllo Cups

6 frozen phyllo pastry sheets, thawed

1/2 cup (1 stick) unsalted butter, melted

1/2 cup sugar

For the Pistachio Brittle

Cooking spray

2 cups sugar

1/2 cup water

$^{1}/_{4}$ cup salted pistachios (shelled)
Honey, for drizzling

Directions

1. To make the ice cream: In a large, heavy saucepan over medium heat, bring cream, half-and-half, and honey just to a boil, stirring occasionally, until honey is melted and mixture is hot. In a medium bowl, whisk the eggs and salt, then very slowly add 1 cup hot cream mixture to the eggs, whisking constantly (you don't want the eggs to scramble). Pour egg mixture into saucepan and cook over low heat, stirring constantly with a wooden spoon, until custard is thick enough to coat the back of the spoon, about 5 minutes. Don't let it boil!

2. Strain the ice cream custard through a fine-mesh sieve into a bowl and let cool, stirring occasionally. Chill, covered, until completely cold, at least 3 hours. Freeze custard in an ice cream maker according to instructions. (The ice cream will keep in an airtight container in the freezer for up to a week.)

3. To make the phyllo cups: Preheat oven to 375°F. Brush 4 of the cups in a muffin pan with butter, leaving at least 1 unbuttered cup beside each buttered one. Follow the instructions for stacking phyllo on page 155, sprinkling each buttered layer with $^{1}/_{2}$ tablespoon sugar.

4. When you have stacked all 6 rectangles, use a paring knife and small plate as a guide to cut out 4 round stacks. Press each round stack into buttered muffin cup. Bake phyllo cups until golden and crisp, 8 to 10 minutes. Immediately lift phyllo cups from pan, twisting carefully to loosen them, and place on a rack to cool. (Phyllo cups can be made 2 days ahead. Store in an airtight container at room temperature.)

5. To make the pistachio brittle: Spray a large cookie sheet well with cooking spray. Stir sugar and water in heavy saucepan over medium-low heat until sugar dissolves. Bring the mixture to a boil and cook, without stirring, until syrup turns a deep golden color, about 8 minutes. Immediately pour mixture onto the cookie sheet, spreading it out, and sprinkle with pistachios. Be careful: The sugar can burn you. Working fast, use the tip of a knife to gently pull and stretch the caramel into a thin sheet. Let the brittle cool completely and break into large pieces with a knife. (Brittle can be prepared a few days ahead. Store in an airtight container at room temperature.)

6. To assemble the dessert, place a phyllo cup on each plate. Scoop honey ice cream into the cups, garnish each one with a piece of pistachio brittle and a honey drizzle, and serve.

Acknowledgments

I owe a great big thank you to a number of people for their valuable contributions to this book. First and foremost, thanks to my agent, Mitchell Waters. Thanks to my esteemed editor, Christy Ottaviano, and to Amy Allen and the rest of the team at Henry Holt/Macmillan Children's Publishing Group. Chandra Ram read the manuscript with a keen culinary eye and developed most of the recipes, for which she deserves credit. Sara Otterstrom provided insight into the world of television production. The community of chefs and volunteers at Salud! Cooking School in Nashville were an inspiration, as was Michael Pollan's fascinating and important book, *The Omnivore's Dilemma.* Of course, much gratitude and love to AmmAppa, my friends, and my family, whose unflagging support and enthusiasm mean the world to me. Last, but certainly not least, thanks to my readers, who make writing not just possible, but worthwhile.

Go Fish!

GO FISH

QUESTIONS FOR THE AUTHOR

© Anna Williams

KATHRYN WILLIAMS

What did you want to be when you grew up?
Other than a princess? At various points I wanted to be an actress, an archaeologist, a sociologist, an anthropologist, and then a journalist. Now, like my character Sophie, I want to be a chef when I grow up.

When did you realize you wanted to be a writer?
I wrote my first short story in a pink Trapper Keeper my mom gave me when I was about eight. It was about a wild horse named Babbling Brook who got in trouble when the field she used for grazing froze over and then burned (still frozen). What I lacked in basic understanding of the laws of nature I made up for in appreciation for dramatic tension. There wasn't a moment, however, when I went "Aha! I will be a writer, by Jove!" It was a long and twisty road to this point, with a short stopover in journalism first.

What's your most embarrassing childhood memory?
I am still haunted by the time I tried to take my sweater off in preschool, thinking I had on an undershirt. I didn't. I crawled

under a table and refused to come out. My very first wardrobe malfunction.

What's your favorite childhood memory?
Christmas Eve, when my extended family got together at our house, brings back lots of warm fuzzies. Also—the time my family visited New York City right after my older sister moved there. We went to FAO Schwarz and then dinner at the Rainbow Room on top of Rockefeller Center. I had never felt so glamorous.

As a young person, who did you look up to most?
Probably my older sister. She's twelve years older than I am. I idolized her—and my older brother too (by ten years). My mom made him drive me to school and, secretly, I loved it. Taking his little sister to kindergarten every morning probably did wonders for his chances with the girls, so you could say he still owes me one.

What was your favorite thing about school?
I loved art class and English. Grammar I wasn't so wild about (although I am very grateful now that it was drilled into me), but I loved when we got to literature.

What was your least favorite thing about school?
Having to wake up so early. I was always that kid bolting through the door one minute before the bell. To say I'm not a morning person is a wild understatement.

What were your hobbies as a kid? What are your hobbies now?
As a kid I took dance lessons—ballet and then modern—and did an acting camp in the summer. I played the Mad Hatter in

Alice in Wonderland and a soldier in *Babes in Toyland.* When I reached middle school, I started playing field hockey and lacrosse. These days I like to hike and do yoga. My boyfriend and I both enjoy cooking, which is lucky as we also both enjoy eating.

What book is on your nightstand now?

I have a stack of them. (I tend to read several at a time.) Right now I'm reading *The Edumacation of Jay Baker* by Jay Clark, sent to me by my lovely editor after I expressed interest in it on Facebook (a neat trick I will try again); a book on Anastasia Romanov as research for a book idea I'm working on; *Amelia Anne Is Dead and Gone* by my friend Kat Rosenfield; and *The Baker's Daughter* by Sarah McCoy.

How did you celebrate publishing your first book?

Champagne at lunch with my editor! And a lot of squealing.

Where do you write your books?

In my bed. It's my favorite place to write, although it's dangerous when I'm sleepy.

What sparked your imagination for *Pizza, Love, and Other Stuff That Made Me Famous*?

My increasing love of food, cooking, and *Top Chef.* I started writing it on a trip to Napa Valley.

Can you cook? How did you learn?

Yes, ma'am! When I was a kid, for my dad's birthday, my mom used to let me make dinner out of one of her big fancy cookbooks, which was kind as it really meant a huge mess for her to clean up. I lost interest in college but then got back into it when I lived in New York. Realizing recipes were just a jumping off point was a revelation. Now I learn by trial and error. I also volunteered at a cooking school in Nashville for a couple years. I learned a lot from the chefs there.

What's your favorite meal you make yourself?
I make a really good flatbread with figs, prosciutto, red onion, and gorgonzola. Sounds weird but tastes heavenly.

If you could order your perfect meal at a restaurant, what would it be?
Not fair! That's like asking me to pick my favorite book: impossible. Honestly, I'm that person who asks the waiter what's best on the menu. I like it when the chef decides. Just give me fresh and seasonal and let the ingredients speak for themselves.

Do you watch reality television? What are your favorite and least favorite programs?
I love the cooking competition shows, like *Top Chef, Chopped,* and *Cupcake Wars,* because they require talent. I think the world could do without the *Real Housewives.*

Which reality TV program would you most like to go on, if any?
I'm waiting for the day they make a reality show about novel writing. *Next Top Author* or *Project Story Arc* or something. The world's most boring reality competition ever! Even then I'd pass, I think. I make a spectacle of myself enough in everyday life. I don't need it filmed to embarrass my family too.

How are you similar to Sophie?
Sophie's a little headstrong, like myself. Once she sets her mind to something, there's no looking back.

What challenges do you face in the writing process, and how do you overcome them?
The hardest part of writing is editing. I've found it's important for me to take some time away from what I've written so I can come back to it with fresh eyes. I also struggle with pacing, so outlines help me with that.

What makes you laugh out loud?
My friend tells pirate jokes that are so bad they're good.

What do you do on a rainy day?
Curl up, read, watch movies, and sleep.

What's your idea of fun?
Zip-lining with spider monkeys in the rainforests of Bolivia. Or just having friends over for dinner.

What's your favorite song?
Another impossible one. When it comes to music, I have broad tastes. Since I moved to Nashville I've gotten more into bluegrass. There's a band called the SteelDrivers. I love just about all their songs. They're stories set to music.

Who is your favorite fictional character?
Ignatius J. Reilly from *A Confederacy of Dunces* is quite entertaining.

What was your favorite book when you were a kid? Do you have a favorite book now?
Shel Silverstein's *Where the Sidewalk Ends* was one of my favorites, but I try not to play favorites.

If you were stranded on a desert island, who would you want for company?
Someone with multiple personalities.

If you could travel anywhere in the world, where would you go and what would you do?
I am dying to go back to Greece. I also really want to see Cuba and Morocco. I'd explore. I'm not much of a sit-on-the-beach kind of girl. If you saw how pale I was, you'd understand why.

If you could travel in time, where would you go and what would you do?
I would travel to the 1990s and buy the publishing rights to the Harry Potter series.

What advice do you wish someone had given you when you were younger?
I wish I'd taken a year after college to just travel and explore. And in more general terms: relax.

What do you want readers to remember about your books?
Every book is slightly different, but I want them to remember a character, a feeling, maybe a laugh or two. I also hope that my books cause readers to look at themselves or at a situation and feel more connected to the world around them—that feeling of, "oh, other people feel or think this too."

What would you do if you ever stopped writing?
I'd go to culinary school.

What should people know about you?
I will be ten minutes late.

What do you like best about yourself?
My ability to laugh at myself. It's essential not to take yourself too seriously, especially as a writer.

Do you have any strange or funny habits? Did you when you were a kid?
I type so much on the computer that sometimes I find myself ghost-typing what I'm saying or thinking. Weird, right? When I was a kid, I was a sleepwalker. I had so many sleep issues that I actually went to a sleep clinic in high school. It felt a little bit like an alien abduction.

What do you consider to be your greatest accomplishment?
My friendships.

What do you wish you could do better?
Write. It is always, always, always a process of honing.

What would your readers be most surprised to learn about you?
I hate olives. I've tried. I really have. I just don't like them. Writing about Sophie's enjoyment of them was an exercise in pure fiction.

you'll find laughter, love, and wit in these great reads!

AVAILABLE FROM SQUARE FISH

Get Well Soon
Julie Halpern
ISBN: 978-0-312-58148-0

The Sweetheart of Prosper County
Jill S. Alexander
ISBN: 978-0-312-54857-5

The Espressologist
Kristina Springer
ISBN: 978-0-312-65923-3

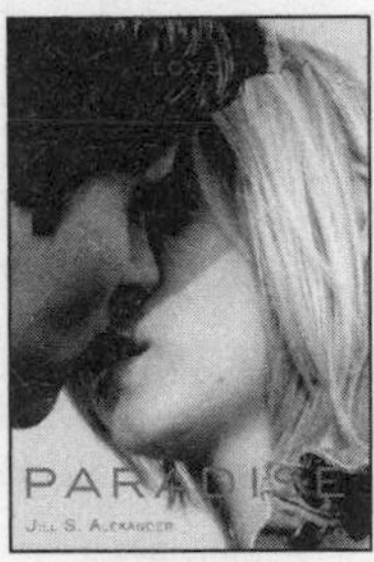

Paradise
Jill S. Alexander
ISBN: 978-1-250-00484-0

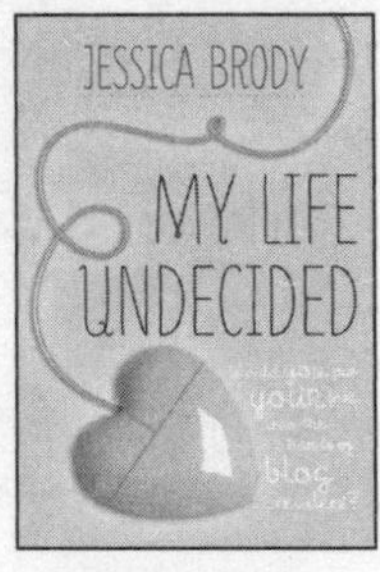

My Life Undecided
Jessica Brody
ISBN: 978-1-250-00483-3

Into the Wild Nerd Yonder
Julie Halpern
ISBN: 978-0-312-65307-1

Flirt Club
Cathleen Daly
ISBN: 978-0-312-65026-1

The Poison Apples
Lily Archer
ISBN: 978-0-312-53596-4

The Karma Club
Jessica Brody
ISBN: 978-0-312-67473-1

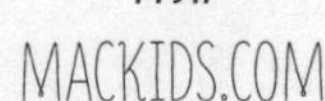